THE DARKEST MASTER

by

RHEA SILVA

Published by **CHIMERA**
ISBN 9781780807904

Chapter One

He stood alone on the headland. On the very edge of the crumbling cliff. One misplaced step and he would plunge down to be pounded on the rocks by the relentless sea. But no - this wouldn't happen - not to him. He wished it would, weary to the depths of his being, out to the far reaches of the universe and beyond.

The sunset cast a blanket of fire across the sky and the water, though yielding to the night-clouds spreading relentlessly to swallow up the remains of the day. It was cold. Even his sheepskin jacket couldn't warm him. The wind was rising, whipping back his hair, pressing the denim jeans against his thighs. Darker it became, and darker still, but he saw something in the bay. His heart sank as he recognised it.

He resisted, crying aloud, 'No, not again!'

It was useless. Nothing could prevent him from taking part in that dread ritual. He could feel the earth dropping away. Could see it fading from sight. Then his feet encountered that all too familiar pitch and toss of a vessel running before a storm. He hated it, but it also gave him a sense of belonging.

Kirsty heard Martin come in. She checked the time. It was after 2 a.m. Where the hell had he been? Unable to sleep, she had lain in bed, watching trash on late-night TV. This was happening frequently lately. True, they had been living together for two years and perhaps the gilt was wearing off the ginger-bread, but even so?

He had always been secretive, but she had put this down to English reserve, trusting him, believing in him, until recently. She had tried to talk about it, choosing her words carefully and keeping it light, but he had made excuses to escape. Both were very busy people with many demands on their time, but it hadn't been like that at the start. He had found the time for her then. Not her first lover, but never before had she had a permanent relationship. She enjoyed the cosy feeling of intimacy, the idea of being a couple, invited to the same gatherings, writing Christmas cards signed from both of them. She would have liked to be married to him, becoming Mrs Cooper, but he had never suggested this.

She scolded herself for being paranoid. There was probably some perfectly innocent explanation. But the gut instinct that is part of the female psyche refused to listen. Reason had nothing to do with it. It was their inborn goddess knowledge that told them when they had been betrayed.

She got out of bed and shrugged on her towelling robe.

She slept naked but needed to be covered to confront Martin with any kind of aplomb. It was just too easy to let desire overtake her. He was very adept at lovemaking, having a degree in it or so she always thought. She had paused sometimes to wonder where he had learnt it. He was cagey about his past, older than her by half a dozen years and, as they say, he had 'been around.'

He heard her and shouted, 'You still awake? Want a drink or something?'

'No thanks, I'm swimming in tea,' she tried not to add, but couldn't stop, 'you're late. Where have you been?'

He strolled into the bedroom, carrying his cup. Kirsty's heart seemed to turn over in her chest, as it always did when she looked at him. He was a stunner, all right, and she the envy of many women who knew them. Tall and slimly built, he had brown hair, hazel eyes set in a tanned face and a smile that could charm the birds right down from the trees. In his early thirties, he was experienced enough to use his assets to full advantage, yet retained a kind of boyish charm - frank and open on the surface but calculating and devious beneath. Or so Kirsty was beginning to recognise, though denying it rigorously to begin with.

'Darling, you sound like a nagging wife.' He set the coffee on the nightstand, then took off his coat and unbuttoned his white shirt, baring a chest that was well muscled and sprinkled with hair.

Kirsty's resolve began to waver. The sight of him undressing was enough to blind her to everything except her need to screw him. *Get a grip!* She ordered herself. 'You haven't answered my question.'

He looked across at her and his smile had become a little fixed. 'I told you that I was going to visit Myra Moore. You know, the one who has that painting for sale. A Gainsborough, or from his school anyway. I'm trying to get her to lower the price.'

She was well aware of this. If she was into buying and selling antiques, then Martin was an expert on pictures. It worked well, the shop below the flat an excellent showplace. Both belonged to her, but that hadn't presented a problem, until now. Mrs Myra Moore was another matter entirely. A rich widow who had inherited her husband's collection. All the fine art dealers were sniffing around, anxious to lay their hands on some of these prizes. And none was keener than Martin.

'Did it take that long to persuade her?' Kirsty was trying to be calm, difficult when she recalled Myra's chic. Middle-aged she may be, but money provided her with the best designer clothes, personal trainers and plastic surgeons. A tempting prospect for an ambitious man and Martin was nothing if not ambitious.

'I told you I was meeting her. She invited me to her place for dinner.'

'Just dinner? What was on the menu? Were you the starter or maybe the dessert? I'll bet she couldn't wait once you were in her clutches.'

He frowned. 'Now you're being silly. I'm only interested in that painting.' He had stripped to the buff and came towards her, an Adonis who worked out in the gym and had a seamless tan, due to sessions under sun-lamps and trips abroad on business.

'Are you, Martin? Doesn't the alluring Mrs Moore appeal to you?' Kirsty trembled as his hands came out and pushed open her robe, cupping her breasts and rolling his thumbs over her nipples.

He answered her question with another. 'Why should I want her when I have you, darling?'

Was it true? She wondered, while thought was at all possible. Or was she a jealous bitch so lacking in self-worth that she assumed he'd find everyone else more attractive? He was with her now, with a fine erection that he wanted to put in her. She had got to believe him or go stark, raving mad!

'Oh, Martin,' she sighed, accepting defeat. 'What am I going to do with you?'

'Take me to bed, honey. And I'll make you forget all this nonsense. You've been a naughty girl, suspecting me like that. I think you need to be spanked.'

His words thrilled her. He had taught her the meaning of going over his knee, arse bare, and receiving the flat of his hard palm. At first, she had disliked it, but soon found that the flame shooting through her backside communicated with her loins and clitoris. Now he was persuasive and plausible and she was in lust. This was not the time or place to push the argument further. She didn't want to, anyway. All she desired was to accept her punishment and lie with him in the depths of their four-poster, to exclude the world that was peopled with Mrs Moores, all wanting to get their claws into her man.

He sat and grabbed her roughly, forcing her to lie, face-down across his lap. She could feel his erect cock pressing against her side. He made her wait, anticipation heightening her desire. Then, just when she thought he wasn't going to hit her, his hand contacted her bare bottom with full force. She yelled and bucked, but he had only just started. Slap after slap rained down until she was sobbing, the hot tears dripping, her struggles having no effect. She couldn't escape him.

Then, abruptly, he tumbled her to the floor, and strode to the bed, leaving her to crawl after him. Her buttocks were on fire, but so was her sex. Naked, she wound her limbs around him, blood rushing as he caressed her in that magic way she enjoyed so much. His lips were on her breasts, sucking, toying, rousing her to such a pitch that she moaned and squirmed against him, wanting him to transfer his mouth to her cleft and bring her to bliss.

But there was one thing that intruded. It was nothing really, except that he was, if anything, too clean. 'You've already showered,' she whispered, this sensible thought impinging through the pain and passion.

'Nonsense, sweetheart. You didn't give me time, although I always want to be fresh for you. Tonight I simply can't wait.' His skin smelled of body spray, soft to the touch under the coating of fuzz. That, along with the personal odour of his hair, should have been slightly overlaid by masculine sweat.

There I go again, souring my enjoyment, she mourned, and pushed the suspicion that he had showered elsewhere to the back of her mind.

The very fact that she was unsure of Martin heightened her excitement. He kissed her lips, stopping any further talk, his tongue meeting hers in a dance of desire. His clever fingers teased and tormented her nipples, an answering need echoed in her clitoris. He knew what she wanted but kept her waiting, prolonging the ache, making it rise and rise till she was begging him to satisfy her.

His cock was so hard that her former fears abated. Would he have been so aroused if he had come from screwing someone else? She knew him to have a formidable appetite, always up for it and usually wanting more than one orgasm, but she really had no solid grounds for suspecting him. She squashed her uneasy thoughts and abandoned herself to pleasure. It was as if her suspicions had sharpened her desire. Her stinging backside added to the sensation, tingling all through her pelvis to her clitoris.

He stretched beside her, kissing and fondling, and she ran her hands over the length of him, those muscular limbs and that hard-packed belly, the thick bush beneath and the rod of his penis standing proud. He moved, slid down and settled between her legs, fingers parting her labia and concentrating on her swollen clit. He wetted it, then subjected it to a steady massage. Kirsty lay prone, the warmth radiating from her sensitive organ, spreading to her lower back and her womb. It gathered force, impossible to stop, rising in wave after wave, each one more intense than the last, until she was hurled high and toppled over the peak, the feeling so exquisite that she blacked out for a second.

She came to herself, wanting to share the pleasure with him, eager to take him into her body, but he pulled her face down to his groin, muttering, 'Suck it.'

His excitement was echoed within her. She wanted to come again and started to tongue him, her mouth working on his pulsing shaft, feeling it swell, hearing his gasps. She sucked harder, her cheeks caving in as she milked him. His hips jerked, his cock convulsed and semen spurted into her throat. She swallowed, but it continued to flow, dribbling across her lips and down her chin and bedewing her hair.

'Jesus Christ!' he murmured, rolling away from her, his deflated cock resting across his belly. 'That was something else!'

Kirsty cuddled against his shoulder. 'Am I the best fuck you've ever had?' She intended it to sound playful, but meant every word.

'Of course, petal.' He was half asleep, but sounded sincere.

She settled down beside him, trying to ignore the pain in her arse, then pulled the duvet over them and slept deeply, waking around eight, knowing she would have to get a move on if the shop was to open at nine.

The space beside her was empty and she swung her legs out of bed, following the sound of Martin's voice. He was talking on the phone and she stood outside the part-opened door of the lounge, hearing him say,

'You really shouldn't ring me here. Use my mobile and don't make it so early.' The caller answered and Martin chuckled. 'You wicked slut! Whatever gave you that idea? All right. On your head be it. We'll try it out next time we meet. When will that be? Give me a time, Myra. Okay, tonight it is, and if you must play with yourself then think of me when you're coming. Did I enjoy the shower with you? Need you ask?'

He hung up and spun around as Kirsty crossed the threshold. His face betrayed his guilt. He turned defence into attack. 'Were you spying on me?'

She no longer had the strength or even the will to go on. 'I want you out of here at once. Do you understand?'

'But, Kirsty... darling... what's wrong?'

'Just get out,' she repeated wearily, but her tone of voice told him that they'd reached the end of the line.

'So, you've finally got rid of that sleaze-bag.'

Kirsty had finished crying for the time being and was now sniffing into a tissue. She glanced across at her friend, Gina. 'Have I done the right thing?'

'Absolutely! No doubt about it. I never liked him, and he tried it on with me, you know, even though you and I are best mates. I told you about it.'

'I know. I wouldn't believe you.'

'I suppose he lied, said that I'd come on to him?'

'He did, as a matter of fact.'

'There you are then. He was jealous because we were so close.'

They were in the kitchen, that homely place where so many consultations had taken place, but never one as life changing as this. Kirsty had phoned Gina as soon as Martin had packed a bag with the announcement that he'd send around for the rest of his personal stuff and sort out what was his in the showroom.

'I'll bet he's already installed at the *Maison* Moore.' Kirsty couldn't stop the bitter tears welling up again. 'Lucky old her!' Gina poured Kirsty another cup of tea and set it on the pine table. 'You're well rid of him. Who's minding the shop?'

'Andy.'

'Good. You can rely on a queen, can't you? They understand what we girls go through regarding men.'

'One of us.'

'Indeed.'

Andy was another close friend. He helped in the business and was totally together, unless, of course, he'd had a row with his latest beau. Then he went to pieces and displayed the emotional side of his nature - plus, plus. No one could be more dramatic than him when he put on his Bette Davis act. Just as well it was plain sailing with his current lover at the moment, and he had offered his support in every way, saying, 'I know, girl. Men are beasts and only after one thing.'

Gina perched herself on one of the stools, heels hitched on a lower rung. She took a sip of coffee and then gave Kirsty a searching glance. 'Where do you go from here? The property is yours, I take it? You didn't do anything stupid like making him a partner, did you?'

Kirsty couldn't take in the cold facts. All she could see was a future bereft of Martin. She shook her head. 'No, there's nothing legally binding.'

'Good thing you didn't get married or you'd be in trouble deep. He'd claim half of everything.'

'I don't want to stay here. Can't face running into him or having friends say that they've seen him and how well he's doing.' Kirsty buried her head in her hands.

'What's the alternative?'

Kirsty knew that despite her rather unconventional appearance and retro way of dressing, Gina was a very practical person when it came down to it. Stunningly beautiful, with long straight hair of a deep red hue and a figure to be envied, she had built up a substantial clientele, giving advice and working with fine materials in her capacity as an interior designer. Heart-whole, she had men if she wanted them, then dropped them like hot cakes if they became too clinging or expected her to be. An independent woman, and she intended to stay that way. No one was ever going to break her heart.

Kirsty came to a sudden decision, 'I'll put this place on the market and make a fresh start somewhere else, far away from here.'

'Right. That's it. As long as this isn't a means of getting back at Martin. Maybe you should think about it for a few days.'

'No. I can't bear to be in the same town as him.' Kirsty knew that she might weaken if he called in and tried to soft-soap her.

Gina got to her feet and came over, putting her arms round Kirsty and hugging her. 'Fine. Put on some slap and we'll go and see an estate agent. All right?'

'Yes,' Kirsty sniffled, taking strength from her. 'Who knows? I might decide to come in with you on a new venture. This town isn't what it used to be. "Fresh fields and pastures new," eh? We can do anything we fucking like! Not called the Glimmer Twins for nothing. You get ready and I'll tell Andy to hold the fort.'

Within two months, Kirsty was in the throes of packing. Her property had been in demand at the price she wanted. She could have got more, but had let it go to Andy who, along with Alec, his new, more mature lover, had wanted to take it on. The legal side had gone through swiftly, keeping Kirsty busy with no time to brood. Martin had angrily demanded stuff he had stored there, and removed the rest of his belongings.

Gina had sent Kirsty out while she coped with him. There had never been much love lost between them and she had followed him round the premises like a hawk, insuring that he didn't take anything other than that which he legally owned.

Kirsty had decided to move to Cornwall. She had been on vacation there as a child in those halcyon days before her parents split up, her father, James Armstrong, moving on with his mistress. Her mother, Val, had remained in the family home until Kirsty came out of university with a knowledge of antiques that stood her in good stead when she set up her own business. Now mother was in America with her toy-boy and Kirsty kept in touch by e-mail. She could have been jealous of Tony, mother's junior by twenty years, but saw how radiantly happy she was, becoming a girl again under his influence. The arrival of a menopause baby half-brother had healed the breach, but she felt very much on her own.

'Cornwall sounds fine,' Gina agreed as they poured over a map. 'All those hunks riding the surf, all those artists going there for the scenery, to say nothing of rugged fishermen battling with the waves. I might leave here and come with you.'

'I'll form the advance guard.' Kirsty gazed around her sadly, about to leave the familiarity of her home. It was daunting, but a comfort to know that Andy would be living there and she could call at any time.

'We'll come down for the weekend maybe,' he promised tearfully when the morning came for her departure.

'I shall miss you.' She gave him a big hug. 'We'll keep in touch and I know you'll make a go of it here. Alec seems very keen.'

'Oh, he is, and faithful, too. Loves me to bits, and he has money. What more could an old queen want? But it won't be the same without you.'

Gina had said goodbye the night before, and Kirsty put a couple of cases in the boot, and the lap-top on the passenger seat and started her car. She had a map, plus details of several properties sent to her by a Cornish agent whom she had found on the Internet.

It was some time since she had travelled so far alone, but she was glad to shake the dust of Bath from her feet. Thanks to the motorway, it no longer took hours to reach Devon and then cross the Cornish border. She stopped for lunch, sensing the certain magic that this county exerted on whosoever dared enter its mystic realms. She had felt this in childhood and it possessed her again on this, her first visit as an adult. She tried to rationalise it, but couldn't. It was just an awareness of a land steeped in legend, almost a separate country from England. It had monoliths and burial mounds, Celtic crosses and stone circles. For a moment she forgot the ever-present pain in her heart as she made her way to where she had booked into a pub that offered bed and breakfast.

Thank God for the Net, she thought as she reached the fishing village of Lanyon Bray and drove into the cobbled courtyard of *The Pig and Firkin*. The inn lived up to its advertising, very old and quaint, and she could well believe that it had once been the haunt of smugglers. She picked up her handbag and the lap-top, locked the car, walked in and up to the bar.

She was greeted by a stocky man with a rugged face and twinkling blue eyes. He was in his late forties and personable, giving her a warm smile as she said, 'Kirsty Armstrong. I believe you're expecting me. We've spoken on the phone.'

'Ah, yes.' He held out his hand. 'Brian Webley, the landlord. You must be tired after that long drive. Would you like to see your room? I'll have your bags sent up.'

She gave him her car keys while they exchanged pleasantries. Then he called over a plump, fresh complexioned girl who conducted her upstairs, saying, 'I'm Meg. A student working during the break from college.' They walked along a panelled corridor. 'Just phone down if you want anything. Are you staying long?'

'I'm looking for something to buy - a shop and living accommodation.'

'Moving down, are you? Cool. It's my hometown.' Meg unlocked a door and stood back. 'You'll find everything you want in here, clean towels and the rest. Give me a bell if you need to. Dinner is served from seven-thirty onwards. The porter will bring up your luggage.'

When she had gone, Kirsty went round the room and en suite like a cat feeling its way into new surroundings. The atmosphere was bland. No ghosts there, all banished by a succession of overnight guests mostly in happy, holiday mood. She missed her four-poster, but that was in store with the rest of her possessions. Instead there was a brass bedstead of Victorian vintage, spread with a patchwork quilt. The view from the window was of jumbled rooftops, with a glimpse of seascape beyond.

Kirsty was weary, but instead of sinking into the mattress and sleeping, she undressed completely, anticipating a shower. She caught sight of herself in the pier-glass, the dealer in her noting that it, too, was Victorian, with a bevelled mirror and mahogany stand. Then her attention focused on her body. She had lost weight lately, too much crying and rushing about trying to leave her past behind her. She was five-foot four inches, with a slim waist, rounded hips and very passable breasts. At least, so several men had told her. Never Martin, of course. He had liked to keep her in her place.

She swept up her corn-coloured hair, holding it on her crown and posing, turning this way and that. Not bad, she decided. I'll take Gina's advice and not be so sparing with make-up. Summer is coming and I'm bound to be able to sunbathe, already have a solid base tan from hours spent in the May sunshine. It's vital that I get a place with a south-facing garden. Money won't be a problem. Some of my loyal customers have promised to keep in touch and Cornwall's resorts pull in plenty of trade during the Season.

For the first time since that fatal day when she had discovered Martin's infamy, a tiny flicker of hope warmed her heart.

The shower was modern and she stood in the stall, guiding the jet over her body. It was relaxing and delicious, but stirring, too. After soaping herself and rinsing, she was aware of a slow burn starting in her loins. It signalled the need to masturbate. Kirsty directed the jet towards her pubis, parting her legs a little, so that the water played on her clitoris. Her dammed feelings burst through. They had been stultified by the shock of Martin's betrayal. Now they came to life with a vengeance. She threw back her head, wet hair streaming, aware of the jets striking her everywhere, like a thousand tiny tongues making free with her body. Nowhere more so than on her eager clit that was many times more sensitive than the male equivalent - the penis.

The shower was lined by mirror tiles and she could see herself, a wanton woman using a hand to spread her labia and allow that swollen nubbin to stand forth. She massaged it, dipping down into her sex juice and anointing it. The feeling was almost too much and she used a lighter touch, but couldn't entirely stop. She opened herself wide, wider still, using the jet then reverting to her knowing fingers, giving herself pleasure so acute that she came in a rush, moaning and shaking, her hand still cradling her mound as the feeling passed. She sighed deeply and wanted to do it again, thrusting her fingers into her vagina as if they were a large cock. Her muscles convulsed around them. She was thankful that she had packed a vibrator in her hand-luggage. Later, after making an appearance in the dining-room, she would retire to bed and use it, with no one to gainsay her. She began to realise the advantage of living alone.

He sat at the long refectory table in the Great Hall of his manor house. He was not alone. He glanced across at his opponent, the dice coming to rest between them. The ornate candlesticks placed at regular intervals down the polished surface shone on the beautiful features of a man as fair as an angel, who was smiling at him sardonically. That smile marred the perfection, reflected in tiger eyes burning so brightly it was impossible to stare into them.

'She has come.' The timbre of his voice echoed through the room and rose to the arched rafters of the ceiling.

'Who?' The host knew very well, but refused to let hope flare up. This wasn't the first time, and on each former occasion his guest had been highly amused when it had proved to be disastrous.

'A girl... maybe your salvation. It will be interesting to see how this one does. It relieves the boredom, doesn't it? And you must be so bored after all this time.'

'You could do something about that.' He did not hide his bitterness.

'Why do you resent me so much? I'm your true friend, your only friend, may I add. I did you a favour, gave you what you asked, and this is the thanks I get!' The guest's handsome face changed momentarily into something incredibly ugly, but the transformation was gone in a flash.

However, it had been enough to remind his host of his debt and the consequences if he rescinded in any way. He was helpless, bound, tied - with only one slender chance. Despite himself, he wanted to hear more.

'Where is she?'

Again that cynical, mocking smile. 'You'll meet her soon. Meanwhile, let's roll the dice some more. You never win, do you, my friend? But we have forever to play. Time has no meaning here, has it?'

Chapter Two

Kirsty found the estate agent's office in a cobbled street that meandered down to the harbour. There was a sign over the door that read Pickford, Willis and Caldecote. She had contacted them on the Internet and they had sent her details of likely Cornish properties. The office looked eminently suitable, well-established and prosperous. There was nothing seedy about the dimpled glass in the bay windows or the well-preserved antiquity of the building. Even the noisy seagulls who considered it their God-given right to occupy every roof, seemed a little more refined. She applied her thumb to the highly polished brass bell-push by the front door and a female voice through the intercom bade her enter.

She stepped into a tiled hall hung with watercolours of views and a brown dado that cut the walls in half, dark panelled below with William Morris wallpaper above. Her expert's eye noted that everything was original and in keeping, an Edwardian property furnished accordingly. This satisfied her. Nothing irritated her more than having periods jumbled together. Sometimes it worked, but only rarely could the most skilled interior designer get away with it.

Gina would love this, Kirsty thought. It was a pity it wasn't for sale; she'd be willing to pay over the odds for it. The willowy, sandy-haired receptionist looked her up and down frostily before announcing her. A door to the right was opened almost immediately by a tall, rangy man of middle years who smiled widely as he welcomed Kirsty. He was immaculately booted and suited.

'It's a pleasure to meet you, Miss Armstrong.' He ushered her into his office. 'I'm Robert Caldecote. Please sit down and I'll show you what we have on offer.'

Another charmer. Kirsty viewed him with suspicion as she did every member of the male species these days. Even the pub landlord was flirting with her and he had a wife, albeit kept well occupied in the kitchen. Kirsty had gone out of her way to be nice to her when they met briefly. What was it with men? Was it true that their brains were in their balls?

She was determined to keep this meeting strictly formal, though had to admit that there was something attractive about Robert Caldecote. He was older and seemed very dependable and she knew enough about psychology to realise that she was looking for a father figure in this stressful time, therefore needed to be doubly careful.

'Are you familiar with the area, Miss Armstrong?' He sat opposite her, the wide desk between them, and was idling with a pen, passing it between his fingers. His hands were tapering, the nails well manicured. How would they feel caressing my nipples, she mused.

'No. I'm a stranger here, but I know what I'm looking for.' She put aside naughty thoughts, gaining confidence under his kindly regard. 'I had an antique shop in Bath and lived above it. Something similar would be ideal.'

They discussed her price range and he seemed suitably impressed, but, 'We have nothing on our books with living accommodation.' He shuffled through print-outs and handed several over for Kirsty's perusal. 'This shop is in an ideal position.' He pointed out one situated in the main street. 'It gets a lot of tourist trade, but the apartment above is occupied. However, you have enough capital to buy a house as well.'

Kirsty spread her hands in a gesture of uncertainty. 'I'm used to living close to my work. It's much more convenient. I don't want to have to drive there and back every day.'

'You need not be far away, and you'll receive regular rent from your tenants. Should they decide to leave, then you can sell up, if you wish, and move there. Nothing is carved in stone, Miss Armstrong. Things change.'

'Indeed they do.' She was thinking of Martin and how this time last year she would never have dreamed of their relationship collapsing.

Robert gave her a quizzical glance. 'You sound as if you've had an unsettling experience lately.'

Kirsty longed to pour out her heart to him, but common sense held her back. He was a stranger and, moreover, a businessman wanting to make a sale. She shrugged and tried to keep her tone light. 'Life goes on and I want to find a place soon, Mr Caldecote. I hope you will be able to help me.'

He stopped looking at her in a speculative manner, and pointed to the property guides lying on the green leather surface of the desk-top. 'I can arrange for you to view the shop in the High Street, and this cottage is a mere five miles away.'

'When can I see them? All my stuff is in store waiting transport and I'm staying at *The Pig and Firkin*. I'm anxious to get into my own home as soon as possible.'

He rose as she did. 'Of course. I quite understand. How would this afternoon suit you? I can take you myself.'

They agreed to meet at two o'clock, and Kirsty had the uneasy yet vaguely excited feeling that he would have liked to ask her to have lunch with him. In her present state of mind and with that lonely ache in her gut she might well have thrown caution to the winds and agreed.

She couldn't wait to get settled and invite Gina to stay. She missed her humour and wisdom and the shrewd way in which she could size men up. Kirsty felt like a newborn babe thrust suddenly into the cold, frightening world. Oh, she could bid at auctions and be ruthless when it came to striking bargains, but give her personal problems and she went to pieces.

Robert took Kirsty to view the shop. She was impressed by his car, concluding that there had to be money in flogging property. Was there a Mrs Caldecote, and why was she even asking herself this question? But in the seat beside him, she was aware of his pristine white shirt and light-weight suit, closely shaven jaw and stylish hair. He was handsome, no doubt about it, and she intended to ring Gina that evening and tell her.

His knee wasn't far from hers and her skirt had risen, exposing her legs. Cars had that intimacy about them that had been many a girl's downfall, like little, private rooms where sex could take place. It was weeks now since Kirsty had had a man. Masturbation was fine, even better than intercourse sometimes, but she missed the feel of a hard, male body pressing against her, a big cock inside her and strong arms holding her. He had large, capable hands and her bottom tingled as she imagined briefly what they would feel like spanking her. She tried to dismiss the thought, but it persisted and she was glad when they reached their destination.

It was no better in the empty shop. Dusky, and as deserted as if they were the only living beings for miles around. Kirsty found it hard to concentrate, all too aware of this personable man beside her. It was true that the premises were ideally situated for trade. The showroom was large and there was plenty of space for storage and a back entrance. It needed decorating, but that was a minor detail.

'What do you think?' Robert turned to her, standing close, his arm brushing hers. Accident or design? she wondered.

'It looks OK. I'd like to see the flat before I decide.'

'The tenants are there now. They say we can go over it any time.'

He led the way outside to a separate door and rang the bell. At once it was opened by a friendly young woman in jeans and T-shirt who took them up the stairs. The apartment was spacious and well maintained. 'I'm Emma Harvey, and I live here with my boyfriend,' she explained. 'We're planning to buy a house as soon as we can, so you'll be able to move in later if you want.'

'That's fine.' Kirsty immediately took to her.

'This is Miss Anderson, Gary. She's thinking of buying the place.' Emma went over to a lanky, bearded, barefoot man who sprawled on a settee in front of the television, watching a football match.

He gave Kirsty a nonchalant wave and lounged to his feet, grinning. 'Pleased to meet you.'

What was it about the hippy type that appealed to her? Kirsty wondered. She'd met several in Bath and on visits to the ancient town of Glastonbury. So laid back on the surface but needy underneath. Often fresh out of re-hab, anathema to a woman like herself who was short on self-worth. She'd do too much for such a man. Become his caretaker, his mother even. What was that line quoted on the cover of the Carlos Santana album? "Call me mother, call me whore, call me Abraxas."

It was obvious that Emma adored him and was his willing doormat. She probably worked all hours to keep it together while he talked a good job, was into alternative religions, Tantric sex, meditation, Buddhism, the development of his spiritual side. The couch held the contours of his body, suggesting that he spent most of his time there.

Not at all sure that she could cope with the way in which he was eyeing her, Kirsty made small-talk. Afterwards she couldn't remember what it was about, but didn't forget his muscles and tight, sleeveless vest or the bulge behind the zipper of his torn, faded jeans.

On their return downstairs, Robert suggested that they drive the short distance to Tregaskis Cottage. It was along the coast with views of the sea and set a little apart from a small group of houses that had once belonged to fishermen. Higher up towards the headland, Kirsty saw the tiled roof and chimneypots of an imposing house.

'Who owns that?' she asked as he opened the car door and she stepped out.

'It's Rosewood Manor, been empty for a long while and was on our books. Then last year it was purchased by an agent acting for a Mr Dirk Stratten, who moved in shortly after. He's a bit of an enigma, keeps much to himself... a recluse, if you like. The manor is a marvellous old place and they tell me that Mr Stratten has filled it with valuable furnishings and antiques. Perhaps he'll allow you to go over it, seeing that you're involved in such things.'

She breathed in the crystal clear air, a sharp contrast to the city atmosphere she had known. Gulls wheeled and screamed overhead and there was the omnipresent sound of waves pounding the beach. I could get used to this, she thought.

Robert walked her up the path between neat borders edged by cockle-shells. Gravel crunched beneath her toe-post sandals and she was enchanted by the fairytale house with its dormer windows and thatch. The ceilings were low and Robert had to duck in places to avoid the oak beams. It was part furnished, and Kirsty could see at a glance that some of the pieces were old and valuable. She was taken with the place, in a bemused state as she climbed the twisting stairs, roamed the bedrooms and peeped into the attics.

She wanted the cottage and was determined that it should be hers. From one of the upper windows, she looked towards the sea and Rosewood Manor.

'I'll have it,' she announced when they reached the ground floor again. 'Set the wheels in motion, Mr Caldecote, and for the shop premises, too.

'You don't want to mull it over for a few days?'

'No. My mind is made up.'

He drove back to the office slowly, as if he didn't want their meeting to end. They entered the building and discussed the financial ramifications. She didn't quibble, agreeing to pay the asking price for both properties. This may have been foolhardy, but all she wanted was to get her life on course again.

Matters concluded, he accompanied her to the door. They shook hands and his palm was warm and dry, the pressure slightly firmer than necessary. He looked down into her eyes, his own a vivid blue in a tanned face. 'You're a stranger and won't know your way around. Would you like me to take you out to dinner in one of our better restaurants?'

She was startled and withdrew her hand. 'There's one question you must answer first. Are you married?'

He gave a quirky smile. 'You're frank, Miss Armstrong, I'll grant you that. No, I'm not married now. I'm divorced. And you?'

'Single, with no ties.' She wanted to escape out of the door, yet toyed with the idea of accepting his invitation.

'I'm simply suggesting that I help you adapt to your new surroundings.' He spoke so disarmingly that she could feel herself weakening. Surely dinner with this charming man would be preferable to sitting alone in the lounge bar of the pub or watching television in her room and thinking about Martin and her appealingly useless tenant, Gary?

'Thank you. I'd like that.' She smiled up at him.

'This evening? I'll book a table and pick you up around seven. Will that suit?'

'Fine.' She kept her tone airy. 'Thank you, Mr Caldecote.'

'Please call me Robert.' He walked with her to the front door. She was aware of his receptionist watching them and hoped that she wasn't about to rain on that young lady's parade.

It occurred to her that maybe they were having an affair.

Gina was in bed with her latest conquest, a man five years her junior. The older she got, the younger she liked them. Fresh, handsome, with unwrinkled skin, long thick hair, muscular bodies and eager, always-at-the-ready pricks. Sometimes, she liked to see how far she could take her dominatrix role. It was fun to teach them perverse as well as straightforward sex. But there were times when she liked to submit to a forceful master. There were so many wonderful and diverse ways of copulating.

It was late afternoon, the town lying somnolent in the deep bowl that cradled it. Volcanic? Apparently not, according to the experts, but nevertheless containing mineral springs heated by rainwater that had fallen millions of years before. The Romans had settled there, luxuriating in the baths after which it had been given its name. A showplace, Queen City of the West.

Siesta time and she had taken Craig upstairs, leaving the shop in the capable hands of her assistant, long-legged and lanky Kelly who preferred girls to boys. They had fucked as soon as they reached her bedroom. She had stripped, freeing herself from his arms and urging him out of his clothes. Her heart had raced as she looked at him. Lovely body. Lovely boy. He was just twenty. Not their first screw, but she wasn't yet bored with him. She knew herself very well and didn't fall in love. It was too dangerous. Craig could ruin her if she let this happen. She'd lose her self-esteem, independence and clarity of vision. She had let it happen once but never again, very nearly destroyed by the experience.

In the dim light, the sun screened by chenille curtains, she had used her consummate skill to bring them both to climax, her hands, her mouth and her sex working magic, squeezing every iota of pleasure from the experience. She had already taught him about the clitoris, still amazed that so many men didn't even know of its existence, expecting the woman to come when they did. Craig had been a fast learner, delighting in practising this new knowledge on her, thinking himself to be King Cock.

'Jesus God!' he had gasped as he thrust and came, filling the condom with his libation.

And Gina had clenched her inner muscles around him, falling down from the heights, almost blacking out with the force of the orgasm he had given her before even attempting entry.

They dozed in each others' arms, and it was the trilling of the phone that roused her. Now they were curled spoon-fashion, her back to him, his hand coming round her ribs to clasp her breast, his prick buried in the crack of her ass. It was thickening again. He was half-asleep but ready for another bout.

'Bugger!' Gina was tempted not to answer, but she could never resist phones. There might be something tremendously exciting going on at the other end. She'd never forgive herself if she missed it.

She rolled away from Craig who groaned and protested, gripping her harder, his erection full-blown by now. 'Let me go.' She felt him chuckle and tighten his grasp. 'Craig! Stop! It's the phone!' She sat up and grabbed it from its cradle on the nightstand. 'Hello, who is it? Oh, it's you, Kirsty. How's it going?'

'Fine... well. I think it's fine,' her friend's disembodied voice replied. 'I've put in offers on two properties.'

'Wow, that's quick. Tell me more.' Gina lay back against the pillows and Craig feathered his fingers through her bush, parting her labia and inserting a questing finger.

Kirsty talked and talked, telling her everything that had taken place, finishing with, 'And Robert's taking me out to dinner tonight.'

'Way to go!' Gina carolled with a catch in her breath as Craig toyed with her clitoris. 'I want to hear more about him, and who is this Gary you've mentioned? Seems like it's time I got my arse down there.'

'Gary's my tenant... hippyish, but living with Emma, his partner. Robert's tall, dark and handsome, with blue eyes and slightly greying hair and is divorced.'

'And you fancy him?'

'Sort of, though I'm not bowled over, not like I was the first time I saw Martin.'

'I'm glad to hear it. There's no way I want you getting entangled again until I've had the chance to look him over. I'll visit soon. Must keep an eye on you, my girl. Now I've got to go.'

'You've someone there?' Kirsty sounded almost accusative.

'Craig. Remember him? Yes, it's still on, kind of.' Gina wanted to hang up, Craig's insistent finger just too pleasurable. 'I must hang up. He's playing with my pussy. Let me know how you get on this evening. *Ciao, Contessa.*'

Now Gina could concentrate on Craig, shelving her concern about Kirsty. His excitement was echoed in her groin. She didn't want to wait any longer and went down on him, feeling his shaft swelling, her mouth working on his throbbing glans. His moans aroused her even more and she sucked harder, her cheeks caving in. He gripped her hair like a bridle, holding her to him and she milked him, feeling his hips jerk and his cock convulse. His come spurted into her throat, then dribbled across her lips and down her chin and bedewed her hair.

'My turn.' She gave him no respite as she lay on her back and had him position himself between her legs, slurping at her.

After finishing the call, Kirsty sat in her room, her head buzzing. There were so many details to go into. She was thankful to have an acquaintance like Robert who would be in the know, helping her with solicitors and bank managers and all the complications of buying not only one property but two. Resting in the coolness of late afternoon, she began to plan what she would wear that evening and try to decide how to play it if Robert pushed his luck. Would she go to bed with him? Not on the first date. Date? It was hardly that. She was his client. Not the romance of the century, and this was how it should be. She had no intention of becoming embroiled with anyone yet, no matter how personable.

Wishing that she had brought more changes of clothing with her, she took a diaphanous, handkerchief-pointed skirt from the wardrobe and teamed it with a strawberry pink vest-top, low-necked and with spaghetti straps. The effect was pleasing and sufficiently sexy to be interesting without appearing tarty. Not that this mattered much these days, she mused, as she sat at the dressing-table, watching herself critically in the mirror.

The twenty-first century new woman had gone beyond mere emancipation, striving to ape men in talk and behaviour. Kirsty found this sad. It didn't become girls to go out on the pull, getting drunk and shagging anything with a pulse. No way did it bring them fulfilment, if those sick reality shows on TV were anything to go by where the participants washed their dirty linen in public and a smooth-talking, highly paid presenter played God.

Gina managed to maintain the status quo, a feminist yet able to be feminine at the same time. She could be outspoken, even coarse, but her sense of humour and balanced attitude prevailed. Kirsty sighed and wished for the hundredth time that she had half her friend's glamour and poise. It occurred to her that maybe it wouldn't be wise to encourage her to move to Lanyon Bray for she would undoubtedly cramp her style. She pushed this disloyal thought from her briskly. Gina had never been other than generous, helpful and supportive. There wasn't a spiteful bone in her body.

Kirsty wished she was there now as she made her way down to the bar where she had arranged to meet Robert. 'Would you care for a drink before we go?' He saw her and came across.

'Thank you. A Margarita, please.' Kirsty occupied a settle near the inglenook fireplace. The hearth contained a black iron basket big enough to hold logs the size of a man's torso. It was empty now. No need for a blazing fire in this weather, but she promised herself that she'd call in there in winter. It might well become her habitual watering-hole if the landlord got the message and stopped flirting.

She wasn't the only stranger present. Half a dozen holiday-makers were sitting close by. They had North Country accents and were studying maps and discussing a visit to the Secret Gardens of Heligan planned for the next day.

'This makes me feel almost at home,' she said, when Robert returned. 'Bath was packed with tourists at the height of the season.'

'A lovely city.' He put their drinks on the oak table and then sat beside her.

'You know it?' This was heartening. She hadn't realised that she was feeling homesick. 'I was born there, a regular Bathonian.'

'Lucky you. I came to it later. Used to go clubbing at Mole's when I was at University there.'

'That's still terribly trendy, under the high pavement of the Paragon.'

'The very same. My God, how it brings it all back.' Everything he said made her confidence rise. They were both from the same neck of the woods and had something in common. This gave her a sense of belonging, and she would have liked to sit closer to him, but held back. She wanted to know more about him before making any move that might suggest she was interested.

'You must know Walcot Street, where I had my shop.' She sipped the cocktail, that delicious blend of Cointreau and Tequila, and her reserve started to melt. I'm beginning to enjoy myself, she thought.

'I do indeed. There was a bookstall nearby where I'd browse for hours.'

'And Theobald's for the best coffee in the world.'

'How could you leave such a place?' His eyes were bright, his pleasant mouth smiling, showing perfect white teeth. No stranger to his dentist, by the look of it. This pleased Kirsty. There wasn't the slightest hint of halitosis on his breath to mar his kisses. And she wanted him to kiss her, most definitely.

She sensed that he felt the same, drawn to her like steel to magnet, and braced herself for the feel of those lips capturing hers. Then a commotion at the outside door made her draw back. A gang of men came breezing in, occupying the spare tables and crowding round the bar. They brought with them a whiff of salt spray and wore T-shirts bearing Hang Ten logos. Copper-coloured skins and bleached hair, baggy shorts and terrain sandals, it was easy to see that their raison d'etre was riding the waves and dipping into the troughs only to sail skywards again, then skim up the beach on their boards.

'The local surfing club.' Robert sounded sceptical. 'They think they're the bees'-knees, entering competitions up and down the coast, even going as far as Australia to prove their superiority.'

'You don't join in?' Kirsty guessed that he didn't but couldn't help teasing him. He looked none too pleased by this sudden influx.

'No. I like to swim and enjoy the sea, but have no desire to risk drowning or breaking a leg on an unpredictable bit of laminate.'

'They've enviable tans.' She was thinking of Gina and how much she would have relished the view.

'And are very healthy, I grant you.' Robert was frowning and she saw another side of him, the petulant child who would sulk if denied his will. I'll bet he can spit out his dummy just like any other bloke, she decided.

The leader of the surfers spotted them and came over. 'Hi there, Rob, old chap. Long time no see. And aren't you going to introduce me to the young lady?'

He was rangy and broad-shouldered and sported a black beard, not too thick and bushy, but a nice coating over his chin, meeting long sideburns. His hair was long, too, curly as a gypsy's, brushing the nape of his neck and beyond. In fact, he gave the impression of being a Romany, having dark eyes and a devil-may-care attitude. He smiled at Kirsty and she felt the full impact of his almost flagrant masculinity.

'Kirsty, this is Seth Polruan.' Robert made the introductions ungraciously. 'Seth, meet Miss Kirsty Armstrong, who is about to move down here.'

'The pleasure is all mine, Kirsty... if I may?' Seth took her fingers in his and placed a kiss on them, this gallantry belying his raffish appearance. 'Welcome to our community. I'm Cornish, born and bred, and it'll take some time for you to be accepted here, but I'll do my best to smooth the way.'

'Thank you.' She was disconcerted by his attention.

'Do you surf?'

'No.'

'Would you like to try it?'

'Maybe, later, but I'm very busy at the moment. I have a shop to open and a cottage to get in order.'

'If you want any help, come to my place on the harbour. I sell surfboards and equipment from there, and live above it. I know most of the tradesmen around here... decorators, carpenters, the kind of guys one needs when setting up an establishment in a new town. Can I buy you a drink?' He stared at her with those most amazing eyes, slightly upward tilting at the outer corners, a network of wrinkles fanning out as if he spent much time staring into the distance in search of bigger waves or pastures new.

'No, thank you.' She glanced at Robert for support.

He came to her rescue. 'We've got to get going. A table booked at *The Admiral's Arms*.'

'Right. I'll leave you to it.' One of Seth's eyebrows raised slightly as he added, 'Catch you later, Kirsty. Call in at my gaff any time.'

She promised herself that she would, her spirits lifting as she mused on having two new acquaintances who found her attractive - the businessman and the surfer. It was more than just satisfying.

The Admiral s Arms lived up to its reputation for being a five star hotel and having a fine restaurant. Robert was knowledgeable about it. 'Of Victorian vintage, it was once the home of a Northern industrialist, built during the time when Cornwall was being opened up as a holiday resort. St Ives, situated close-by, became the haunt of Bohemian writers, sculptors and artists and gained a rather racy reputation in the old days, as the playground of the advocates of 'free love'.

'How interesting,' she remarked, though aware of the reputation of St Ives.

'Now the hotel belongs to a chain, modernized and improved and fiercely expensive,' he went on. 'You've heard of Harry Ogden, I expect, one of TV's most popular chefs?'

'I've seen him on the telly.'

'Well, he's recently taken this over, ruling the kitchen with a rod of iron. That is when he's not engaged in appearing in a weekly cookery spot on Channel 4, writing a book or adding his rather bizarre charm and acerbic wit to various celebrity programmes.'

'That's right.' Kirsty tried to sound impressed, though cooking wasn't exactly her forte. 'It was really popular among young marrieds I'm friendly with. It's the 'in' thing to throw dinner parties and show off skills you acquired under the on-screen guidance of masters like him.'

'I know him personally,' Robert added, as the maitre d' ushered them to a secluded table in the dining-room. 'I'll introduce you to him later. He's supervising the cuisine tonight. That's one reason why I chose this place.'

She wondered if she was supposed to be impressed as a sparklingly white napkin was spread over her knees by a girl in a black uniform and the wine waiter appeared, hovering on the balls of his feet as Robert perused the list of vintage brews and House specialities. She was no stranger to being wined and dined and Bath was high on the gourmet list, but even so it was some time since she had been taken out like this, not since Martin decamped, in fact. She liked the sensation of wealth and luxury, of being pampered and cherished.

She had a shrewd idea that she wouldn't get this with Seth. It would be down the pub for a beer and packet of crisps, then fish and chips on the way home. To his pad? Probably, where he would expect the ultimate favour.

Would I give it to him? she conjectured, while scanning the menu and listening to Robert recommending this dish or that. The thought of lying beneath Seth's powerful frame so toned and honed by battling with the surf, caused a pleasurable ache in her loins.

'And what do you like to do when you're not selling antiques?' Robert tasted the wine and nodded his approval. The waiter filled his glass and one for Kirsty. 'I'm very fond of music.' She sipped the excellent Chardonnay. 'Have a big collection of CDs of my favourite composers.'

'Which are?' The starter arrived, delicious and fishy and expensive, a treat for the discerning palate.

'The Romantics, mainly. Prokofiev, Tchaikovsky, Stravinsky, Rachmaninov.'

'All Russians.'

'Agreed, but I love Ravel as well, and he was French, some English composers, too... Delius, Vaughn Williams and Benjamin Britain. But best of all I adore Italian opera. Puccini is my maestro. Followed by some, but not all, of Verdi's works. Then there's Wagner. German, of course, and a giant among composers.'

'You've seen *The Ring Cycle?*' He was fired by her enthusiasm, and her own passion for this subject affected her, too, making her tingle with an excitement that was not merely cerebral but sexual. She visualised the magic of listening to the more seductive passages of Wagner's music while indulging in floor-rolling sex with Robert.

'No, but I have a set of DVDs showing the whole of a wonderful performance from the Metropolitan Opera House, New York. Have you seen it live?'

'Oh, yes. Once in Bayreuth during the Wagner Festival and then recently at Covent Garden.'

'Wow!' she exclaimed. 'The whole thing takes four evenings, doesn't it?'

'Yes, and it becomes rather like a party, you occupy the same seats and get to know others around you. There's eating and drinking during the intervals and the atmosphere is electric. Maybe we could go together some time. Fly to New York, perhaps? My wife didn't share my love of music.'

Kirsty was at a loss for words. This was going a bit too fast. But the idea of being escorted to the theatre by this man and possibly sharing a hotel room with him thrilled her, in spite of her reservations.

The excellent food and fine wine acted on her like an aphrodisiac. Robert was becoming more and more desirable with every sip or mouthful she took. He was an entertaining companion, with an ironic turn of humour and she hadn't enjoyed herself so much for ages. The room sparkled with cut-glass and gilt framed mirrors, popular classics provided background music and the light fell from half a dozen chandeliers set at regular intervals along the ornate ceiling. Each table had its own silver candlestick, the muted glow flattering the face of every diner.

'I'd like to do this again.' Robert reached out a hand to touch hers where it rested on the table. At the same time, she felt his knee against hers, hidden by the damask cloth.

'So would I.' She was amazed by her own daring. What on earth would Gina make of this? 'Steady girl! Hold your horses,' she could almost hear her saying.

Nevertheless, his pressure on her knee did not lessen and she wanted more, willing those strong fingers to cruise up her thigh, finding the silky inner skin and not stopping till they brushed against her pubes.

She was roused from her sensual dream by a hearty voice booming, 'Hello, Robert. Have you enjoyed your meal?'

Robert rose, went around the table and shook hands with the tubby man who stood there. 'It was superb, Harry. You just get better and better. How are tricks?'

'Everything's coming up roses. Never realised that the Brits found cooking so fascinating.' Harry laughed and took a chair. He was still wearing his chef's apron and cap and seemed jovial, not the tyrant of his television persona.

'This is Kirsty Armstrong. She's bought two properties here, a shop and a cottage and will be moving in directly.' Robert resumed his seat.

'From London?'

'Bath.' Kirsty was overawed by him. He was so big in the media - such a celebrity - TV, magazine interviews, newspaper articles. Yet, in the flesh, he appeared to be quite ordinary.

'Nice town. Did a stint in the Assembly Rooms not long ago. The Mayor's inauguration ceremony or something. Hired me to do the food. I miss the old Smoke, however. Love London. Couldn't stay down here for very long or I'd stagnate. I wish you well, anyhow. What's your line?'

'Antiques.'

'Very nice. Good luck to you.' He stood up, casting a shrewd eye about the place, noting the behaviour of the waiters and waitresses. He had the reputation of being a hard taskmaster. 'I hope you'll come again.'

'Oh, I shall,' she promised, thinking that Gina would fancy herself in such surroundings.

Harry was about to depart when the maitre d' hurried over, looking for all the world like an agitated secretary bird. 'Mr Ogden,' he cried, hot and bothered about something as yet unknown to the rest of them.

'What is it, Dawkins? Is the house on fire?'

'No, sir, no. Mr Stratten has just this minute arrived. He wants to see you.'

Kirsty glanced across to the doorway. She tried to look away but couldn't, riveted by the man who stood there, tall, commanding, wearing a faultlessly tailored evening suit. It was as if he knew she was present, staring directly at her. His eyes seemed to bore into hers and she was aware of a dizzying sensation, the floor shifting beneath her feet, becoming that of decking on a storm-tossed ship, rising, falling, beset by the sound of crashing waves.

He came nearer, accompanied by another man, as fair as he was dark. Robert and Harry did not move. They were like puppets and the stranger was in control of their strings. Then, 'Good evening, sir. Your usual table?' the maitre d' ventured.

'Yes.' Stratten's voice was low but ringing, with an accent that Kirsty couldn't place. 'Bring the menu after I've spoken with Mr Ogden.'

The evening had been warm but now Kirsty was suddenly very cold. The stranger was perhaps the most handsome man she had ever seen. His companion, too, was outstandingly attractive, though there was something wild about his face and bearing.

Both men were arrogant, lords of all they surveyed. There was an old-worldly mien about them, as if they came from a past age when aristocrats owned slaves and ruled the peasants with tyrannical force. Stratten's eyes were hard and his friend's downright cruel. Yet both of them sent shivers along her spine and into her sex.

As Gina would have said, had she been present, 'I'd give them breakfast in bed!'

Time seemed to have stood still. Kirsty wasn't sure which way was up and which down. It was more than the wine, there was a strange ambience in the air and it emanated from Stratten and his friend. No one else in the restaurant seemed aware of it, or were they in another dimension? *Was she?*

Maybe she had died suddenly? She looked on the floor for her body, but it seemed that she was still inhabiting it, the blood coursing through her veins, nerves zinging, sex eager for *him* - this alien who she felt she had known forever.

Someone was talking - she thought it was Robert - mundane conversation bringing her back to reality. 'The manor house is to your satisfaction, Mr Stratten?'

Stratten inclined his head. 'It suits me well enough. I'm not here often. I have business abroad,' and as he spoke, he kept looking at Kirsty.

She was paralysed under the penetrating gaze of his hungry sea-green eyes. Visions of mountainous waves in storm-tossed oceans filled her mind. She could hear the freezing wind and the creak of spars and the groaning of timbers as a vessel tried to plough its way through the pack ice. Glaciers reared up, and huge bergs forged ahead like juggernauts. And yet, in spite of the blood-curdling cold, the fiery embers glowing in the black pupils of his extraordinary eyes seemed to draw her ever closer, though neither of them had moved.

The impression could have lasted a second or an eternity. She thought she heard Stratten saying, 'We are practically neighbours. Come to me tomorrow evening and I'll show you my treasures,' but she couldn't be sure if his voice reverberated in her ears or in her brain. Whichever it was, she inclined her head and resumed her meal with Robert, while the stranger and his companion moved off with Harry.

'An odd-ball.' Robert refilled her glass. 'His arrival put the local ladies in a flutter, but he doesn't accept their invitations to dinner parties. Keeps very much to himself.'

'Who is that other?'

'Mr Lucian Sauvage. He's often with him, but there again, seems pretty elusive. It gives the Woman's Institute food for gossip. They can't make either of them out. Stratten is generous when they collect for Good Causes, puts the other businesses to shame, but that's all they get from him... a generous cheque... nothing else. No feedback.'

'Do you think he and his friend are gay? Lovers, perhaps?'

'I've no idea. It's quite possible, I suppose, which might account for their reserve.'

'Did you hear him ask me to the manor tomorrow evening?' She awaited his answer with a kind of restrained eagerness.

'I did.' Robert was frowning, as if none-too-pleased with Stratten's invitation. 'Would you like me to come along?'

'No. I shall be all right. I can't wait to take a peep inside.'

'Is that all? You're interested in his antiques, not the man?'

Kirsty could feel herself blushing. 'I'm not seeking another relationship. I'm still trying to recover from the last,' and she gave a rueful smile.

'Ah, is this your way of warning me off?'

'No, Robert. We're friends, aren't we? And we have common interests. Surely, that's enough, for the moment?'

'Of course.' He was once more his gentlemanly self. 'And now might I suggest one of those mouth-watering desserts. Harry excels himself at them.'

Back to normal again, and it was as if Stratten had never existed. When the meal was finished, Robert suggested, 'I'd like to invite you back for coffee. I'll show you my selection of recordings. I expect you're missing yours.'

She wasn't, having brought a player with her and her favourite discs, but had been too pre-occupied to listen to them. Coffee? Was that all he wanted? She picked up her wrap and bag and followed him to the car.

Chapter Three

The entrance to the Club Aphrodite was dimly lit and guarded by wide-shouldered, no-necked heavies with shaven heads and cauliflower ears, incongruously attired in tuxedos. They stood aside deferentially to let Dirk and Lucian pass. The sombre walls of the foyer were decorated with lurid flashes of scarlet. These seemed to be alive, as if powered by lightning. The air should have been hot, but struck those who dared to enter with a weird and intense chill.

Not so Dirk and Lucian. They were at ease in this tense atmosphere, wearing magnificent crimson cloaks with sable collars. These were open down the front, weeping back from their bodies as they walked, displaying their naked torsos, tight black velvet breeches and top boots.

Music seduced the senses, sometimes a cacophony of jagged, ear-splitting sounds, at others whispering of passion and indulgence in everything associated with copulation. Dirk and Lucien strolled into a magnificent room that seemed to stretch forever, the far end lost in he distance. It was wide, too, and filled with people engaged solely in fornicating. Every aspect of sex was the order of the day. Males fucked women, while some went with men. Women made love to women or were linked with creatures that resembled satyrs, half male, half goat with enormous erect phalli sticking out before them and large balls nestling between their hairy thighs.

It was like a fancy-dress party, but with a difference. Whereas in normal, polite society such events would be circumspect, at least until the wine flowed freely, in this instance there were no such inhibitions and the emphasis was on sex from the start. The costumes were elaborate. There were a high percentage of cardinals and monks among the men, even a pope or two, along with pirates, cowboys, knights, sultans and kings. The women and transvestites favoured nuns' wimples or schoolgirls' gymslips. Some strode around in high-heeled PVC thigh boots, flourishing whips and wearing open crotched briefs and basques and thongs. A number of harem-girls in transparent saris acted the subservient role. Every fantasy known to man appeared to be catered for, as well as several so peculiar that they might have come from another universe.

Lucian stalked up the three shallow, red-carpeted steps of a dais and took his place on a throne-like chair. He rested an elbow on one of the carved arms, chin in hand and a brooding expression on his face as he observed the antics of his followers. They paused apprehensively as he scrutinised them, then continued at a casual wave of his hand. Dirk occupied the top step and a waiter brought them drinks. He was a slender, beautiful youth with long ebony hair and a Cupid's bow mouth, the epitome of boyish innocence, until one looked into his amber eyes. They were like bottomless pits, holding a wealth of sinful knowledge.

Lucian slipped a hand into the youth's crotch. 'How are your parts, Adrian?' His voice was husky and low.

'You should know, sir,' the young man gasped, his breath jerky as he came into Lucian's palm.

'Oh, I do. Rest assured of that.' Lucian transferred this tribute to his mouth.

'Welcome, master.' A ravishingly beautiful woman materialized at his side and he did not rise, merely lifting her hand to his semen bedewed lips.

'Well met, Aphrodite. Is business brisk?'

'Never better.' She wound her bare arms round his neck. 'I can't remember a time when there was such an upsurge of interest in cunt and prick.'

'We can thank technology for this.' Lucian's expression was one of deep and abiding cynicism. 'Every vice is so readily available now. One no longer has to go out searching for it. Just click a switch, press a button, and hey presto, one's darkest, dirtiest longings will be satisfied. As with every other invention, the computer can be used for good or ill. But man, being the debased creature that he is, indulges his low-grade lust as usual. God was warned not to create such a creature, but He wouldn't listen to the angels even when they went to war with Him, and look at the result! Conflict, terror, destruction of this most beautiful planet and all because of His arrogance.'

'It's fun though, isn't it? I enjoy the power it gives me. Don't be so gloomy, master. I can see that you need cheering. What is your desire?'

He shrugged. 'Show me something different and entertaining. I have a hard-on that seeks relief. Do it for me and do it now, or you'll suffer!'

'And your friend? What does he need?'

'Something that even you can't supply, cher.'

'Indeed?' She tossed her mass of blonde curls defiantly, annoyed that her prowess was in question. 'But I have outdone the most skilled whores, had more men per session than any of them. Even the Empress Messalina couldn't win over me and she liked nothing better than to challenge the prostitutes of Rome. My record is two hundred and fifty cocks in a night. And you try to tell me that I couldn't find a way to service him?'

He chuckled and pinched her prominent nipples through the transparent garment that barely covered her voluptuous body. 'Even you couldn't satisfy his hunger, though there is one in existence who might, but whether she will agree, not even I can tell. The price is very high.'

Her sapphire eyes narrowed. 'What is she, an emissary from your arch enemy?'

Lucian shrugged. 'Who can tell? Where does good end and evil begin? Are they not opposite sides of the same coin? Beauty or ugliness? Order or chaos? Life or death?'

Close by, a naked woman hung in chains from a crosspiece. A large man dressed as a gladiator, lifted a pliable whip and brought it down across her thighs. She yelled, but her cries changed to whimpers of pleasure as he repeated the blow, and then moved in to palpate her clitoris. Another girl was trussed like a fowl and raised from the floor where she swung backwards and forwards, her genitals displayed for all to see and touch. And they did. Males and females paused to examine her and caress her most private area now accessible to all. She sighed and arched herself as much as she could in her bonds, and those who enjoyed her took pity on her and repeatedly brought her to fulfilment.

Aphrodite snapped her slender fingers and twin nymphets appeared, as alike as two peas in a pod. They were chained together by the ankles, ebony-haired and almond-eyed, wearing minute gold G-strings that barely covered their mounds and had straps that passed between their legs and into their bottom cracks. Their breasts were bare, small and firm with gilded nipples. They advanced to where Dirk and Lucian sat, and pushed aside their robes, making admiring noises as the erect phalli appeared. They acted as if they had never seen anything so amazing, squirming low and applying their luscious red lips to the bulging helms.

They were highly skilled at fellatio, but even so Dirk experienced hardly a twinge of desire, watching them disinterestedly, seeing how their dark heads bobbed up and down and the cheeks of the girl concentrating on him drew in as she sucked at his dick. He felt those lips slurping and caressing, her tongue-tip darting into the small slit, milking it of its jism, but at the same time he stood apart. This had happened so often in the past, with Lucian urging him to squeeze every vestige of enjoyment from existence. Yet he could not lose himself in it. There was something missing, a vital element for which he yearned, a gateway to freedom.

Aphrodite had summoned her cohorts, and they gathered round, watching the master as they chased their own brands of pleasure. The music became louder. A bevy of beauties slithered up and down, rubbing their crotches against poles. Muscular men mounted handsome youths, plunging their cocks into willing rumps. Women lay together, kissing and fondling breasts and cunts, and lovers who got their kicks from straightforward sex, practiced the missionary position, groaning loudly as they reached their zenith. Some women were being roasted; taking one cock from behind and one in their mouths. Some squatted over one cock, took another in their mouths while a third rammed into their backsides. Some were hung by their ankles, their legs wrenched wide apart and satyrs swung whips at the targets thus revealed while the women sucked hungrily at the massive cocks.

Two strapping Amazons were wrestling in a ring, one black, one redheaded, magnificent specimens of strength and power. The crowd were betting on the outcome, circling them eagerly, shouting advice. There was a loud whack and the black contender's nose started to pour blood. By way of reprisal, she tore off her opponent's thong and threw it to the spectators, then grabbed a handful of wiry red pubic hair and yanked at it, receiving a savage kick in the crotch that floored her. But even in the midst of this vicious contest, the wrestlers were handling one another's clefts. In the end, they dropped down, the foxy-hued one sitting astride the black beauty while they brought each other to climax.

Dirk half-closed his eyes and leaned back, his elbows on the dais, legs outstretched. He relaxed, pleasure gradually taking over. He thrust his hands into the girl's hair, drawing her head closer as sexual energy possessed him and nothing mattered but reaching his apogee. It was mounting, higher and higher and he was aware of the almighty feeling that heralded climax. It came in a huge wave, his penis jerking while semen spurted from him.

Two things impinged on his ecstasy - Lucian's bark as he, too, came, and the sudden vivid picture of the young woman to whom he had been introduced earlier - Kirsty Armstrong.

'We'll go to my place,' Robert said as he and Kirsty left the restaurant.

The offer to show her his record collection had been corny she thought as she got into the car, but disarmingly genuine. Anyway, what did she have to lose? Plenty, was the right answer, but the wine had made her reckless, as had the sight of that remarkably fascinating man, Dirk Stratten. She found it hard to put him from her mind. His film star good looks were unforgettable, but it was more than that. There was something about him that called to her, a longing she could not dismiss. It was as if she had known him forever. He had inhabited her dreams, though she had not realized it until seeing him in the flesh. Every hero she had ever fallen for in movies or envisaged while reading romantic novels was encapsulated in this man.

Martin? Who was he? Had she really imagined that he was in love with him? Now she saw it as a foolish infatuation. Dirk had invited her to the manor. Was this true or false? Something deep inside her told her that he wouldn't forget.

The weather had changed quite suddenly, rain lashing he windscreen, and Robert said, 'That's what happens down here. You'll get used to it. All to do with the tide.'

'But it's been so hot. Is this heralding a break in the weather?'

'Could be.'

Robert lived in a converted chapel on the outskirts of Lanyon Bray. It had been tastefully changed from the House of God to the House of Estate Agent. 'You didn't get rid of the churchyard,' Kirsty said as he held up an umbrella and they ran for shelter in the porch and then into what had once been the vestry.

'No, though it's no longer used for interments, but here are people who like to come and remember their lead, bringing flowers and scrubbing the tombstones. They're mostly old and, when they're gone, it'll fall into disuse.' He shook out the umbrella and took her wet wrap.

'Don't you mind being surrounded by corpses?'

He opened the door into the large room that had once been the main body of the church. It made a superb lounge and he conducted her through glass doors at the far end that led into the kitchen and dining room. 'They don't bother me. Neither do the ghosts of past vicars. I sleep like a baby.' He busied himself making coffee, then set two cups on a tray.

'How long have you been here?' She wandered around, admiring the ribbed vaulting and stained glass windows, while every nerve was responding to him. She told herself sternly that she was acting like a sex-starved loony, and admitted feeling the loss of a power-packed cock after being regularly serviced.

'Five years. I bought it when I split up from my wife.'

'Were there any children?' She walked back with him into the main room.

'No. This was one of the reasons for the break. She didn't want babies.'

There was so much left unsaid in this bald statement and Kirsty sensed his disappointment. She wanted to comfort him. Steady on, warned her sensible self. He's only selling you property and isn't some lost soul in need of rescuing.

She sank into the depths of one of the large settees and Robert placed the tray on an inlaid coffee table and then went to operate the stereo. 'You've a huge collection.' She stared at the shelves lined with CDs and videos.

'I've been gathering them for ages. My wife had no ear for classical stuff, so I watched and listened when she wasn't around.'

'And now you can do it any time you like.'

'That's true, but it's lonely. Music is for sharing, don't you agree?'

Chords swelled from the state-of-the-art speakers, magnificent and awe-inspiring. The fine down rose on Kirsty's limbs. 'That's Wagner.' She recognized the piece.

He nodded, pleased. 'The prelude to *Tristan and Isolde*. Have you seen the opera?'

'No, but it's on my list of things to do.'

'It's nothing like as complex as *The Ring Cycle*.' Sound filled the room and she wondered how the spirits of long-gone churchmen were reacting to Wagner's passionate love music. She was aware of something in the atmosphere, not exactly ghosts, but a presence, nonetheless. It made her uneasy. It was as if she was being watched by unseen eyes, assessed by an invisible judge, challenged by an unknown enemy. She gave herself a mental shake, putting it down to the stress of moving and too much alcohol.

Robert came across to sit beside her, not too close, keeping a respectful distance, but it was companionable, and he topped up her coffee cup and talked music. He knew a lot about it. If only relationships could remain at this level, she reflected. They both recognised their attraction to one another, but were taking their time, testing the waters, as couples did in a bygone age and Kirsty liked this. Robert wasn't subjecting her to any pressure. Just because they were alone there was no suggestion that he might take advantage and jump her. He was a gentleman, through and through.

His home was tranquil and she appreciated that.

Living in the pub did not suit her, she was a person who liked her own space and privacy. Robert didn't have to be told this. He sensed it from the start and it gave her a feeling of meeting with his approval and being understood. She kept reminding herself that naturally he would flatter her, for she was a client who was about to spend a great deal of money and his firm would reap the benefits. Even so, the time passed pleasantly and she was on a musical high when she glanced at her wristwatch and declared that she must be going.

'So soon?' He sounded regretful, and the arm that had been resting casually along the settee back, moved to encompass her shoulders.

She didn't pull away. It was pleasant to be held, drawn closer to him and she wanted so much to relax and let him take care of everything. His mouth hovered over hers and she waited for his kiss with a delicious sense of anticipation, every good resolution taking flight. She closed her eyes, her own lips parting.

The kiss never happened. A vivid flash of lightning blasted through the arched windows, followed by an ear-splitting crash of thunder. The chapel shook. Rain beat at the panes. The wind lashed the elms in the graveyard and lighting made the tombs stand out, bathed in an uncanny blue-white glare.

Robert drew away from her. 'Don't be afraid. It's only a summer storm and won't last long.'

'I want to get back. I hate thunder.' Somehow it now seemed imperative that she leave.

'We'll go, just as soon as it passes.'

The words were hardly out of his mouth before there was a sudden cessation of noise. No lightning. Not even the distant rumble of thunder. It stopped raining abruptly. 'Is it always so capricious?' Kirsty reached for her bag.

He gave her a quizzical smile. 'Cornwall is a mysterious place. The natives believe in all manner of strange tales, including that of the Tommy-Knockers.'

'Who're they?' She was nervous, unwilling to go out into the night.

'Ask any retired tin miner and he'll tell you that he and his mates never sang or whistled underground. This annoyed the Little People, the Tommy-Knockers who live down there, tiny creatures with the big heads and wrinkled faces of old men and the bodies of year-old children. It's said that they were often heard tap-tapping in the galleries and the wise miner always worked in the direction of that sound, for there the mineral vein was sure to be rich. He always left a bit of his pasty for them.'

'Every county has its own stories.' Kirsty tried to shake off the feeling of foreboding that threatened to spoil the evening. 'Please take me back to the pub.'

Robert drove her to *The Pig and Firkin*, and they shook hands very formally and he promised to contact her as soon as there was news concerning the properties. The landlord let her in and she managed to avoid answering his jovial suggestion that they have a drink in the bar before retiring. She closed her bedroom door thankfully and switched on the television as she got ready for bed. A popular reality show was on air and she watched it idly.

Her mind was spinning with the day's events, the most outstanding of which was meeting Dirk Stratten. She humped her pillows into a more comfortable shape, and leaned back, her eyes on the telly, the remote control to hand. The show was running in all its banality, then it changed. Dirk's face filled the screen. He looked very different to the man she had met in the restaurant. He was wild, windswept, battered by a storm that drenched and pummelled him as he stood at the wheel of a ship. His eyes focused on her and she couldn't tear herself away. He was shouting something, but it was lost amidst the roar of waves and clash of thunder.

She started and came fully wake. The vision was gone, the screen filled with a football match. Time had passed and she had no idea how much. The match wasn't something she would have switched to. She didn't like football. She sat up, confused and uneasy. What did her dream signify? She took her diary from the bedside table and opened it at the right page. She always kept an account of daily happenings, be they never so trivial.

Now she wrote, *Good day. Have decided on two properties. The estate agent, Robert Caldecote, is a dreamboat, divorced and solvent, so it seems. He appeals to me. But not as much as my neighbour-to-be, a weird bloke called Dirk Stratten. He's intriguing and so is his friend, Lucian Sauvage. What a pair! Like something out of a Bronte novel. Bet they are into all sorts, maybe cocaine and S&M. Now there's a thought! High time Gina came down and gave the place and its inhabitants the once over. I'm sure she'd go a bundle on Seth Polruan, a real-life surfer who walked into the bar tonight. I must look him up. He'll know the local builders and decorators and I shall need things doing when the sales have gone through. There was a freak storm and Robert scared me with tales of the Cornish piskies. All rubbish, I know, and yet sometimes I wonder.*

She laid her diary aside and snuggled down, though keeping the telly on and the bedside light burning. Since Martin had departed, she found it hard to sleep and disliked her empty bed. As the blues singer, Carol King, had once written, bemoaning the loss of her man, *The bed's too big, the frying-pan's too wide.* Kirsty knew all about that.

She focused on tomorrow, resolving to visit Seth and try not to concentrate too much on whether or not Dirk would honour his promise to have her visit Rosewood. Sighing, she regretted the complications of existence. Here she lay, young, not bad looking, solvent and without baggage, yet there was no man with her, making passionate love and adoring her. It just wasn't fair! She cupped her hand round her pubis and introduced her middle digit, caressing the tip of her clitoris, but even this proved to be no diversion, so she gave up and concentrated on getting to sleep.

Kirsty stepped out into the brilliant sunlight. Cornwall was at its best with no hint of a stormy side. Now it advertised its legendary self, making her think of King Arthur and Tintagel and the famed Round Table.

There were fishing boats and yachts anchored in the harbour, and the cobbled alleys were already awash with tourists. The car park was filling up, private vehicles and coaches disgorging further trippers. Kirsty could feel the sun burning her bare shoulders. She had used lashings of protective cream and hoped to deepen her tan before Gina arrived. They were friendly rivals in sunbathing, each determined to out do the other. This was all the more reason for getting established in her cottage garden. Surely Robert would have a completion late soon?

She resolved to visit his office that afternoon, but meanwhile decided to get better acquainted with the local talent in the form of Seth. She was heading in the right direction. There were several shops and cafes lining the quayside, and it didn't take her long to find his store. It had two big windows and a double door that was opened encouragingly. Goods were displayed in baskets on the pavement. Toe-post sandals in all colours and sizes jostled shrimp nets and fishing lines, sou'westers and peaked caps and, above all, every gadget to appeal to the surfing freak.

Kirsty went in, admiring the multihued bathing towels, miniscule swimwear and a variety of shorts in all sizes. Wetsuits hung against the walls and surf boards took pride of place, as long and sleek as prehistoric crocodiles. The shop was full of women buying postcards, gifts and peppermint rock, and males asking about hiring equipment, fancying themselves as beach-boys. Some hope, she thought, for most of them had beer-guts.

And there was Seth, as chunky, dark and sexy as she remembered. He smiled across at her and she pretended to be absorbed in checking out the bikinis, taking one down from a rail. It consisted of three mock leopard-skin triangles that covered the nipples and the Mount of Venus and nothing else. She didn't really need another, having several in her possession but, 'How much?' she asked, when Seth sauntered over.

He examined the price tag. 'To you, dear lady, fifty quid all but a penny.'

'Daylight robbery.' She replaced it on its hanger.

'Worried it won't fit you?' He raised an impudent eyebrow as he looked her up and down.

'Not at all. I have a couple already, and they are even smaller.'

'Why bother? Why not sunbathe nude?' He was leaning closer, making her aware of his tan and his muscles and the outdoor smell of him. It was an alluring combination. She knew it, and so did he.

'I do, when I can, but it isn't always convenient.'

'You can use my backyard any time. Perfect privacy. Anything goes.'

'Outside here?' She couldn't quite believe this for it seemed to be surrounded by buildings.

'You got it. There's a little corner that belongs to me. Fine and secluded. Shall we go down there now?'

'Who'll mind the shop?'

'I've got assistants. Come on, Kirsty. I dare you. I'll even give you the bikini to try out, free of charge. There's an offer you can't refuse.'

He was ginning down at her, challenging her and she had never been one to pass up a dare. The sun was hot, and there was absolutely nothing she could do to forward her plans at that precise moment. Why not go with him and let Fate decide the outcome?

Taking her silence for assent, he went to the back of the shop and issued orders to a couple of gangling lads who were aspiring surfers, only too glad to work for him. Then he disappeared momentarily, returning with a carrier bag containing a bottle of Coke and a packet of sandwiches. He grabbed two towels from the rails and also the bikini. Kirsty followed him through a rear door and down a side lane. It meandered along behind the large shed where he manufactured the boards, and came out on a narrow stretch of harbour. Seth was right. It was secluded, screened by a wall on one side and a trawler on the other, anchored and riding low until the text tide.

'That's mine, too,' Seth pointed out. 'My dad was a fisherman, but I only use it to take folk on trips round the bay.' He set the carrier on the concrete, squinted up at the sky and arranged the towels so that they faced the sun. 'Right, now... get 'em off.'

Kirsty had worn a flowing dress, a tanga and no bra. It was a matter of seconds and skilful application to get into the bikini without baring her pussy. She put on the bottom, knotting the ties at the sides and hesitated as to whether to bother with the cups. Most people went topless these days, but Seth made her feel shy. She settled it in place, hiding her breasts though deploring the fact that she would now get strap marks.

She rolled up her dress and put it in her hold-all, then used this as a pillow. Seth's hideaway was a real suntrap and she applied lotion, put on her dark glasses and stretched out on the towel. The concrete was hard, but no matter.

Seth did the same, stripping to a thong. He was bronzed all over. Scorning screening oil, he went to the harbour edge, leaned right over, scooped up a handful of water and splashed himself. 'There's nothing like salt to bring on a good tan.'

'Aren't you worried about harmful rays?' It was patently obvious that he wasn't.

'Nope! I'm used to it,' and with that, he spread out his towel beside her and lay there, his shoulder brushing hers.

'I really don't know what I'm doing here with you.' She squinted at the sky through her shades, very aware of him.

'It's my irresistible charm.' He reached out and took her hand in his. 'We're going to shag soon. It's written in the stars.' He suddenly reared up, leaning over her, his face coming ever nearer. Then his mouth descended towards hers, but she covered his lips with her fingers.

'I don't know a thing about you. Are you a married man? Have you a long-term girlfriend? I never poach on other women's preserves. I know how much that hurts.'

'I'm free as air.' The laughter lines deepened at the outer corners of his gypsy eyes. 'No wife, no girlfriend, but plenty of tourist chicks ready to jump into my bed.'

'That's not very nice,' she reproved, though without moving from the circle of his arms.

'I don't pretend to be nice, but at least I'm honest. If you want nice, then stick with Robert. Did he fuck you last night?'

'No, he didn't, and it's none of your damned business. And get off me, you're blocking out the sun.'

'Sorry!' He rolled away, though still grinning wickedly. 'You're as prickly as a hedgehog. What's wrong? Feeling frustrated? I can soon cure that.'

Kirsty chose to ignore him, and he was silent. She slipped into the half-dream state brought about by the sun. She could feel the blessed heat on her skin and pushed down the bra straps, wishing she was alone so that she could remove it altogether. Yet all the while she was aware of the current flowing between her and Seth. It was like a white-hot wire, drawing her to reach out and touch him. She sighed and shifted position restlessly, the peace of the morning ruined.

'What is it?' He moved closer until they touched, shoulder to shoulder, hip to hip. 'Why don't you let me screw you?'

She opened her eyes but was unable to see his face clearly through the glasses. Her nerves were taut as bowstrings and yes, she admitted it, she needed sex most desperately. But why this one and not Robert? *It's the bad boy again*, she admitted. The rogue, the vagabond. They are most appealing. It's a paradox, the spice of danger, the uncertainty, the challenge to turn the reprobate into an honest citizen, at which time, of course, you'd completely lose interest in him.

As she made no answer, Seth gently removed her bikini top, baring her breasts to the rays. Her nipples crimped and he fingered then licked them, causing mayhem in her loins. He threw one muscular leg over her thighs, and she was instantly aware of his hard penis. She didn't respond, though wanting to raise her hips and press against it.

She started to struggle. 'We can't. Not here. Someone might see us.'

'Who? There are no windows this side of the workshop. In any case, my guys wouldn't dare interrupt me. I've got 'em well trained. Come on. You know you want to.'

The trouble was, he was right. She did want to. The heat, the smell of the ozone, the feeling of freedom, coupled with her own desire, was almost too potent to resist. He slipped a hand down the front of her bikini bottom, cruising through her pubic hair and landing on the seat of arousal. Kirsty shuddered, wanting to stop him, yet overwhelmed by the need for him to continue.

'Don't.' Her protest sounded feeble.

'Don't what? Don't go on or don't stop?' he teased, gripping her thigh between his, making her fully aware of his erection.

'Well, well,' Lucian crooned, gazing down into the pool. Within it was mirrored the scene on the quay. 'What do you make of that, Dirk?'

They were in a cave linked to Rosewood by an underground passage carved in the rock. The rugged walls had a phosphorescent glow. A single ray of sunlight struck the pool through a crevice in the roof.

'I don't like it. First Robert and now this oaf. What is she? Some kind of sex maniac?' Dirk's brows drew down in a scowl. 'I thought you said she was to be mine?'

'So she is, if she'll have you once she understands the deal.' Lucian's tawny eyes glinted as he stared at the small image of Kirsty reproduced in his makeshift scrying glass. 'She's gorgeous. I wouldn't mind a dabble there myself. What d'you say? Do we share her?'

If it had been possible, Lucian would have lain dead at Dirk's feet, struck down by the violence of his glare. 'You know bloody well there's nothing I can do to stop you.'

'You can't, maybe, but she could.' Lucian continued to look at her. 'See how she presses her pussy into his hand. She's so wet and wants to come very badly. Shall I let him bring her off?'

'No!' Dirk rapped out. 'She is for me. You promised.'

'Calm down, dear boy,' Lucian chuckled and picked up a small pebble from the cavern's sandy floor. He dropped it into the pool. Ripples obscured the vision.

'Fuck me! What was that?' Seth shouted as a boulder hurtled by, missing his head by a fraction of an inch. He leapt to his feet, staring in the direction of the warehouse.

If it's those bloody kids on the roof again, I'll have their guts for garters. They could have killed me. Come on, get your things together. We're going.'

Kirsty sat up. 'What's happened?'

'I was nearly concussed, that's what.' Seth was struggling into his baggy shorts. 'Why are you smiling? It's not funny!'

'I'm not smiling.' She pulled a straight face. 'It's just so sudden. A missile out of the blue. Where did it come from?'

'I don't know but I'm going to find out. No one interrupts me when I'm on the job.'

Kirsty gave a mental shudder. His phraseology left much to be desired. Perhaps she'd had a lucky escape. But even so, her clit was throbbing and every inch of skin seemed to be crying out for caresses. With her dress in place again, she trudged back to the shop. Seth was in a bad mood.

'There's no need to go off on one,' she snapped when they reached the main door.

'Oh, hell.' He calmed down, giving her a rueful smile. 'I'm sorry, babe. I was really enjoying it. Now I've got a boner that'll stay hard until I get the chance to have a wank. We'll give it another go soon. OK? Let's have your number and I'll ring you.'

He's certainly down to basics. Not much of the romantic about *him*, Kirsty thought as she wrote it on a piece of paper and handed it over. She left him then, meandered round the Charity Shops looking for bargains and then had a solitary lunch. Her mood had turned gloomy. There was no way she enjoyed living alone.

Gina might extol the virtues of being able to do what you like when you like, but Kirsty needed to be part of a twosome. Sadly she watched young lovers holding hands and married couples sharing simple pleasures with their children. She found a corner of the beach, stripped to her briefs and slept in the sun. She might have called in on Robert, but couldn't face another man and further frustration. He would phone her if he had any news. As for Dirk's invitation? She tried not to think about it.

She woke after a series of muddled, rather menacing dreams and could tell by the position of the sun that it was time to go back to the pub. For what, she didn't know. To phone Gina and have a chat? To find out if Dirk had called there or enquired about her? She checked the messages on her mobile but there was nothing from him. And why should there be? He didn't know her number.

The only thing she wanted was a long, leisurely soak in a bathtub. She was hot and sticky and the sand had adhered to her sun-oiled skin. Lanyon Bray was compact, everything within walking distance, and she soon reached the pub. Before going to her room, Kirsty found Meg and ordered a pot of tea to be sent up. No matter how humid the climate, the English always relished this beverage and she smiled to herself as she threw down her hold-all and got out of her dress. The cool air struck her and the shady room was a delight. The tea arrived and she drank a cup before entering the bathroom.

She rubbed shampoo into her hair, then rinsed it off in the washbasin. Her every movement excited her, as if her nerves were wired. Seth had left her hanging on the edge and her sexual lips were still swollen, her clit unsatisfied. The tub was filling with warm, perfumed water, foamy bubbles forming on the surface, the mechanism humming gently as she switched on the jets. She smoothed back her dripping hair and her eyes focused on the fascinating triangle of her fork reflected in the mirror. The floss was darker than that on her head and crisply curling, with that distinctive central line edging the crack.

She lowered herself into the bath, lay back in the heavenly water and parted her legs slightly, lifting her pelvis, exposing her delta. She held the lips apart with her hand, admiring the hard pink head of her clitoris. She pointed one of the jets towards it, gasping with pleasure as the stream hit the prominent tip.

It was a delicious sensation and she ran the water up and down, arching her pubis, longing for more yet wanting the sensation to last for ever. To relieve the ache and prolong the pleasure, she turned off the spray and smoothed her hands all over her body. Herb-scented gel completed the luxurious feeling and she managed to forget her worries, aware of nothing except her body and its needs. Before long, she could not refrain from attending to her genitals again. Her womb ached, her swollen lips demanded attention and her clitoris throbbed.

She touched it lightly with her fingertips and it was almost too much, very nearly toppling her over the brink and she didn't want this to happen, not quite yet. Experience had taught her how to play with it, massaging it till she was very nearly there, and then holding off, letting the feeling die back so that she might work it up again. She had met only one man who understood how to excite a woman. This was Martin and he had used it as a weapon, keeping control of her by denying her completion sometimes, insisting on spanking her first.

She leaned her head back against the rim of the bath, tormenting her clit, making it wait, and the sensation intensified. She wanted it to last so much, and yielded to the voice in her head that said, 'Get dressed first then, if Dirk doesn't get in touch, you can rub yourself furiously and bring on your orgasm.'

She succeeded in holding back, and left the tub, drying herself on a fluffy towel and turning her attention to the problem of what to wear. The floating skirt of last evening would do again and she teamed it with a white vest top that showed off her tan to perfection. She concentrated on her make-up, using a darker base, more mascara and eye-shadow than usual and a luscious poppy red lip-liner. Her hair flowed around her shoulders like a silk curtain, and the throb between her legs was becoming more and more demanding. She sprayed herself with an exotic French perfume that held all the scents of summer.

She was about to raise her skirt and give in to that little tyrant nestling in her delta, when someone knocked on the door and Meg's voice said, 'There's a car waiting for you, Miss Armstrong.'

Of course there was. Dirk hadn't forgotten. Kirsty flew downstairs to be met in the bar by a tall, cadaverous-featured man wearing a dark uniform and a chauffeur's cap. 'Mr Stratten sent me to fetch you,' he said, his voice deep and cultured.

She followed him and there, outside the pub, was a shiny black limousine. The chauffeur opened the rear door for her and she entered its interior. It smelled of leather and wealth and decadence and she revelled in it. Within seconds, she was on her way through the twilight to Rosewood Manor.

Chapter Four

Kirsty regretted her impulsive acceptance of Dirk Stratten's invitation. She knew little about him. Just because he was the most dishy man she had ever seen didn't necessarily mean that he was to be trusted, quite the reverse in fact. He might be a serial killer or a rapist.

Seated in the plush interior of the car she worked herself into a panic, almost tapping on the glass that divided her from the driver and demanding that he return her to the pub. Curiosity prevented her, along with a large dose of pride. She'd show them that she wasn't afraid and could handle the situation. It got harder to hang on to this as the car left the main road and entered a winding lane. There were no street lights and the ledges on either side were thick. The trees met overhead, their branches interlacing.

She clutched her purse nervously, peering through the windows but unable to see far. The headlights pierced the gloom. The chauffeur handled the wheel confidently and she told herself not to be silly. Obviously this private road led to the manor. There was nothing odd about that. Then why, oh why, did she keep remembering the tart of the movie, *The Rocky Horror Show?*

The lane opened out and became part of a gravelled drive. Before her loomed the great bulk of the house with lights shining at the windows. As far as she could see, it was a Tudor mansion built back in Queen Elizabeth's reign. She caught a glimpse of gabled roofs and conical towers and chimney pots silhouetted against the night sky. The antiquarian in her rejoiced. What an opportunity to explore an historic place! She forgot her forebodings and stepped out quickly when the chauffeur opened the car door for her.

He had braked at the bottom of a flight of wide, shallow stone steps that led up to a front entrance sheltered by a portico. It stood wide and a tall figure was outlined against the glow of light. Dirk started to descend towards her. Her heart gathered pace, thumping in her chest as she stood there as if frozen. He towered above her, his face shadowed as he took her hand, bowing slightly in that formal, oddly old-fashioned way of his.

'Welcome to Rosewood.' His accent was alluring, making her think of gallantry in the courts of medieval kings, of troubadours and knights and damsels.

She smiled, unable to find a suitable response. He seemed not to expect one, simply escorted her up the steps and through the massive door into a vast entrance chamber. She was wise enough in architecture to recognize this as the hub of the house. The Great Hall where once the family had feasted. If the owner had been a magistrate he would have held sessions there to settle disputes, put criminals on trial and discuss village matters and various issues concerning the serfs enslaved to him.

She could picture Dirk as the feudal lord, and while deploring the system that had once existed she found herself wanting to bow down to him.

He held out an arm courteously and she slipped a hand into the crook of his elbow. He led her into the Hall and across to a smaller room. 'I've ordered dinner to be served here.'

The walls were panelled in dark oak and decorated with crossed pikes and swords and tattered banners from battles fought long ago. Suits of armour stood in corners, their helmets holding blank eye-sockets.

The table was already laid. Silver cutlery sparkled in the light from candles set at intervals down its length, six in each elaborate branched holder. There was a magnificent flower filled centrepiece with carved and gilded nymphs and shepherds depicted in a rural setting. Kirsty guessed it to be eighteenth-century and worth a fortune in a top class auction saleroom.

Apart from the table, the rest was of breathtaking splendour, hung with landscapes in gilded frames and tapestries, too. Venetian mirrors flung back the scene repeatedly. Priceless rugs were scattered over the highly polished oak floor like islands on a calm sea. Kirsty could have been in the seventh heaven of delight were it not for her apprehension, and the annoying thing about it was that she really had no need to fear. Dirk was the perfect host.

'Please be seated.' He pulled out a chair for her at the head of the table, next to his own.

He took his place and at once the strange chauffeur appeared, now changed into an evening suit. He held a wine bottle and poured a measure into Dirk's goblet. After swirling it around and sipping it, Dirk nodded. 'A superb vintage, Barend. Bring another bottle from the cellar after you've served Miss Armstrong.' Barend inclined his head and her cut-glass flute soon held the red liquid. 'Here's to you.' Dirk toasted her and she returned the gesture.

Barend made a silent-footed retreat and she asked Dirk, 'Where is your friend tonight?'

'Lucian? He has business to attend to. A very busy fellow with little time to himself.'

'You live here alone? Doesn't it worry you rattling around in this great place?'

His eyes were keen as he viewed her in the candlelight. 'No. I'm a solitary person, Miss Armstrong.'

'Call me Kirsty.' Such formality was touching, but she wanted to get closer to him in every way, her lips burning to have him kiss them.

'That's a nice name.' He set his glass on the table. 'Tell me about yourself, Kirsty.'

She talked throughout dinner, a delicious three course meal worthy of Harry Ogden. It was as if once started a dam burst within her. She couldn't stop, filling in every detail of her life, even things she had not thought of sharing with anyone. Dirk made little comment, listening intently while he ate. She realized that she knew no more about him than when they had first met, whereas he was now in full possession of her history, including her unfortunate affair with Martin.

Barend took away the empty plates and brought in the dessert. It equalled anything she had eaten in the best restaurants. 'Who prepared all this?' The house was so quiet that it appeared to be empty of staff.

'Barend is in charge. I leave everything in his capable hands. May I help you to some more wine?'

Again the block that left her baffled. She lifted the glass to her lips and decided to be more direct. 'Where did you live before you came here?'

'I own many properties all over the world.'

'Really? Were these inherited or the fruits of your labours?'

'Shall we say that they came my way?' His lips smiled, but his eyes were guarded.

'How fortunate.' She found his answer a little too glib.

Was he a con man involved in tricky business deals, running casinos or even a drugs baron? He must have a great deal of money. 'Have you a wife and children?'

'You ask a great number of questions but, if you must know, I have no family, no kith and kin, no wife.' He dabbed his mouth with a snow-white napkin and leaned a little towards her. 'I think it's time I showed you some of my treasures.' He rose and extended his hand. 'Come with me, Kirsty.'

She could no more refuse him than she could stop breathing. There was a mesmerizing quality about him and she seemed to be moving through a dream as she followed him. They passed into a reception area big enough to be a ballroom. From there he took her into the library, a quiet place for scholarly contemplation. It was lined with glass fronted bookcases holding leather bound volumes of great age and value. The big bay windows had deep embrasures and were draped in heavy velvet curtains with tiebacks, and tassels twelve inches long.

The light and airy sitting room came next, where once the ladies had gathered to sew and gossip. There was a games room complete with a billiard table. The walls housed hunting trophies, including a mounted tiger's head and that of a wild boar and a stag. Guns were stored in racks. It was a strictly masculine den where exaggerated tales of bravery and daring could be recounted over and over.

'You like to hunt?' Kirsty couldn't believe it of him. He didn't seem the hunting, shooting, fishing type.

His words proved her right. 'It isn't my favourite form of entertainment. I didn't furnish this house. I bought it from its former owner, lock, stock and barrel. His family had lived here for four hundred years, but he was a gambling addict, lost everything and had to sell up.'

This explained much. 'I see.' Her tone indicated that he considered he had taken advantage of another person's misfortune.

He picked up on this. 'Do you, Kirsty? And what is it you see? An unscrupulous, selfish person? A male who needs a mate? A loner no one understands, but you fancy that you might?'

He looked so angry that Kirsty wanted to take flight.

She stood her ground, outfacing him. 'There's no need to be so rude. If you don't want me here, then I can phone for a cab and leave.'

His expression softened. 'I didn't say that. You haven't seen the rest of the house.'

The tour continued, up a grand staircase, along numerous passages, into rooms that had obviously not been used recently and through a Long Gallery where once the occupants had strolled or played bowls on wet days. It was hung with family portraits, none of them depicting Dirk's ancestors. He was as much a stranger there as Kirsty. The house had been wired for electricity and every corridor was lit by lamps placed along the walls. The chambers had central candelabra and side lighting.

The Master bedroom excelled everything else in magnificence. Each item was exquisite, hand picked by Dirk to enhance his sleeping place. The bed was huge and hung with crimson curtains. The furniture was black with age and priceless. The carpets were oriental and worth a king's ransom. The dealer in Kirsty longed to own these precious things and either keep and gloat over them or sell them on the open market.

He looked at her and laughed. 'I can read you like a book. You're estimating the cost, aren't you?'

She brazened it out. 'Something like that. It's my trade, don't forget.'

'I don't. You've told me all about it. Is this the most important thing in your life? What about love?'

This sudden change of mood took her off guard. 'Love? What has love got to do with it?' She rounded on him sharply, rattled by this unusual individual.

There was something in his eyes that alarmed her, a sudden hungry craving that belied the coolness of his manner. He shrugged her question off. 'Nothing and everything.'

He approached the large fireplace. Its hood rose to the ceiling and the mantelshelf was supported by Titans and carved with acanthus leaves. The iron basket was empty now, but in winter it could blaze with logs. The vision of being in his bed in the firelight was enough to banish every sensible thought from Kirsty s mind.

For a moment he stood there, looking down at the grate, one foot braced on the brass fender. Then he leaned forward and touched a wooden rose that was part of the ornamentation. There was a whisper of sound, so soft that she could hardly believe the evidence of her own eyes as a panel slid open to his right. A dark aperture yawned beyond and a rush of chilly air gave her goose-bumps.

He looked at her. 'The house is riddled with secret passages. I'm only just beginning to discover all of them. Are you brave enough to come with me?'

Every sensible part of her urged refusal, but the pride that she was leaning to find in herself refused to be eaten. She stepped towards the opening. 'Will you go first or shall I?'

His lips curled into a smile. 'I'll lead the way. The steps can be treacherous.' He reached inside the low doorway and flicked a switch. A light came on, showing her a spiral staircase that twisted down, lost in gloom. He ducked his tall head and began to descend. Kirsty allowed.

It was like being on the set of some corny horror movie. She half expected to see Frankenstein's monster at every bend. It was cold and damp and she wished she had brought her wrap. Dirk retreated steadily and she hurried to keep up with him.

She wanted to ask him to wait for her. No way was she going to do that and have him think she was afraid. At the bottom of the stairs she saw him just ahead. The passage had grey stone walls and an uneven floor. Low voltage electric bulbs gave off a yellowish uncertainty. He stopped and unlocked a door. It was arched and made of solid wood and had rusty hinges. The light sprang on as he indicated that she should enter before him. She crept inside, every hair on her body seeming to tingle. This was an alarming and wildly arousing situation. What was he going to do?

The room was like a cell and equally bleak, but its contents left her speechless. There were icons and statues and golden objects of great rarity. Paintings by masters, church altar pieces, rich fabrics by the bale and relics from Ancient Egypt. Dirk threw back the lid of a brass-bound chest and she was dazzled by the contents. Not only was it filled with coins, but also held a variety of precious stones. These had been worked into chains, necklaces, pendant earrings and bracelets. He scooped up a handful and held them out to Kirsty.

She took them. She had never seen such gems. He propelled her to where a mirror stood, its ebony frame serpentine and convoluted. She saw herself reflected as he stood beside her and draped her in jewellery till she resembled an empress from some lost civilisation.

'Perfect,' he muttered, his eyes glinting like the emeralds that adorned her throat.

'Did all these come with the house purchase?'

He gave a bark of sardonic laughter. 'No. These were acquired by my sweat, blood and tears. I have many more, both here and in my other properties, to say nothing of bank vaults worldwide.'

'You don't need all this wealth. It's obscene that one man should own so much when there are people starving to death in war torn countries.' She snatched off the jewels, almost flinging them at him. 'Why don't you give some of it to charity?'

'Stop lecturing me. I would far rather it went to the woman who consented to become my wife.'

'I shouldn't think that would be difficult. Most women would give anything to own a quarter of this.' She looked round her at the glittering array. It seemed tawdry and vulgar.

'No doubt, but there is one stipulation.'

'And what is that?'

'She must love me for myself alone and be prepared to die for me.'

Kirsty laughed, too confused to think clearly. Why was he displaying this stuff to her? Was he hoping to impress her? Was it a childish way of showing off? 'This sounds terribly overdramatic, Dirk.' She wanted to bring him down. He was just too confident.

'It's true.' He came closer and she was so very aware of his height and hard-packed muscles, his dark, brooding face and cynical smile. They were alone there in that remote place and anything could happen. He brought all her deepest, darkest fantasies to the fore, and she didn't even like the man!

She could feel herself getting damp between the legs and despised her own weakness. The very sight of him made her nipples peak and her clitoris throb. 'Have you shown me everything... your riches and power? I'd like o leave now.'

He shook his head. 'Not quite yet, Kirsty.' He placed a hand on her bare arm and her skin tingled, the fine down rising all over her body.

It would be undignified to struggle and she did not want to anyway. He propelled her through another door and into a larger room. It was like a vault. Braziers lit and warmed it, but this couldn't dispel its sinister aspect.

She could only guess at the purpose of the objects there, delving into memories of magazines and porn videos devoted to S&M that had belonged to Martin, and things Gina had told her about. There was a crosspiece from which handcuffs dangled. A vaulting horse stood to one side, complete with straps. Racks held a variety of whips, paddles, flails and canes. More manacles and leather restrainers hung from hooks.

The chill that raced through her was at odds with the heat gathering in her pussy. 'Was this designed by you?' She could not bear to look at him.

'It was left by the gambling man. He got his kicks from it.' There was a thread of amusement in his voice.

'You've never used it?' Somehow she didn't believe that he hadn't. The pieces of the jigsaw were falling into place. He and his sinister friend would be into kinky sex. A spasm of jealousy racked her.

'Sometimes.' It was hard to get information out of him.

'So you've had women here... girlfriends?'

'If you can call them that. Would you care to try?'

'No... I'm not into that kind of thing.' Memories of Martin's spankings made her pulse leap.

'I don't think you're being truthful. Aren't you itching with curiosity? I can give you sensations you've never before experienced.'

This was the point at which she should have declined and left abruptly. She did neither, hypnotised by his powerful presence.

He stared deep into her eyes and she could feel herself drowning in the blackness of his pupils. He knew her so well. There was nothing she could keep from him. She found herself in his arms, the solid baton of his cock pressing against her. She was a helpless prisoner of his will, but more than that was her pity for the sorrow and yearning that possessed him. There was something he was begging her to do, his need for love overwhelming. This was no reprobate, no selfish seducer but a lost soul in desperate straits.

'What do you want of me?' she whispered into the darkness of the hair that coiled about his ear.

'Nothing... I can't ask you... it wouldn't be fair...'

'Please. Tell me.'

'No. Hush. For your own sake I'd prefer that you hated, not loved me.'

He slipped off his tie and bound it round her eyes. What are you doing?' she gasped.

'Indulge me.'

Unable to see, her other senses became keener. Deprived of movement by the iron grip of his hands, she was aware of the personal smell of his body, overlaid by expensive aftershave. Her skin prickled as he found the zipper at the side of her skirt. The silky material slithered to her feet. He pushed up her vest top and unfastened her bra. The chilly air made her nipples crimp. His fingers entered the side of her panties and combed through her bush, finding the hard nub between her slick wet lips. She cried out at the pleasure of it.

He abandoned her clit, swung her around and pushed her forward until she could feel hard wood pressing into her belly and breasts. She guessed it to be the whipping post. In an instant he had slipped manacles over her wrists and fastened them to it.

'Stop it, you idiot! What the hell d'you think you're doing?' She tugged at her bonds to no avail. 'Stop acting so weird.'

He ignored her and pushed down her panties. There was a harsh, metallic click as he snapped cuffs around her ankles and attached them to rings. Now she was spread-eagled and helpless. Fear made her shake, but it was not only that - it was mixed with the desire to find out what he was going to do next and if it included fucking.

The blindfold was uncomfortable, the knot tangling with her hair, but the worst part was not being able to see him and judge what he had in mind. If the eyes are windows of the soul, then she had no way of telling if his was beautiful or ugly and twisted.

'Take this damn thing off!' It was more of a command than a plea. He gave no answer and the heat of his body was suddenly withdrawn. She waited, strung out, vulnerable. Then pain shot through her as his palm connected forcefully with her bare buttocks.

'You bastard!' she shouted, though roused by the familiar feelings of pain and desire.

He slapped her for a second time and, had she not been chained, she would have danced with fury. 'You have a lot to learn, Kirsty. I shall teach you.'

'Too late, Dirk. I was initiated by Martin. He liked to punish me.'

'But not like this. I shall be your first master.'

For an instance there was silence then, with a swish, a whip contacted her flesh. Kirsty yelled, her body jerking involuntarily. The shock of it did not fully register before it was joined by a second lashing. She had never experienced such pain. It stung, flamed through her, and spread to her loins. Her very helplessness caused strange sensations inside her.

She cried out, 'Stop! Stop!' Yet, deep within her, she acknowledged him. Her master. Her lover. The man she had been waiting for throughout her life.

Twice more the whip descended, then she felt his fingers entering her vaginal lips from the rear. She expected his touch to be intrusive, but she was juicy and ashamed of this admission of lust. He spread her dew over her clit and started to drum on it. Kirsty moaned and ground her pubis against that tantalizing touch, the stripes on her flesh burning like fire.

He undid her bonds, freed her eyes, spun her around and captured her mouth with his, tongue probing deeply. Thrills chased down her spine into her womb and she wanted to feel him inside her, a stranger who she hardly new. This was not her style. She was usually cautious, but what she felt for him was an emotion like no other.

He was excited, his cock swelling behind his fly. He changed the rhythm of his stroking, the sharp staccato on her delicate little organ becoming a languorous caressing from stem to tip. He massaged the engorged lips on either side, bringing her closer and closer to bliss, her hungry clit standing up like a miniature cock.

Then he did the thing for which she had hardly dared hope. He knelt before her, parted her thighs, held open her cleft and licked the pink flesh between. He drew her clit between his teeth and gently nibbled, then subjected it to a vigorous sucking. He stood up and moved to her breasts, biting her nipples into hard, aching points. When she was quivering with need, he moved lack, bent and thrust his tongue inside her.

It wasn't enough. She needed a long, thick phallus to probe her after she had been brought to fulfilment. Dirk seemed to know what to do, either by instinct or experience. He raised himself, pushed her back against the wall and opened his pants. His erection jutted out, larger than she had expected. She wanted his touch on her clit, but he pushed into her, lifting her off her feet, his hands clasped around her hips, soothing the smart bequeathed by the lash. She settled on his cock, feeling the hot helm butt her cervix. He withdrew, circled her entrance again and entered. Kirsty squirmed, trying to find his cock root, her clit aching for contact. Dirk pulled out, slipped a hand between her legs and she was certain that this time - *this time* - he would give her release.

She couldn't believe it when he took his hand away and stood back from her. She wanted to cry with frustration and disappointment. She was burning with desire, aching for orgasm. He had brought her so close to the peak and then abandoned her.

'Why did you stop? What is it with you? Do you enjoy this kind of tease?' She had never felt so humiliated, wanting to cover herself as quickly as possible. She retrieved her clothes from the floor.

He leaned against a stone pillar, zipper closed, arms folded over his chest, long legs crossed at the ankles as he watched her coolly. It was as if he had never touched her.

'I was demonstrating how sex can be a pleasure fraught with dissatisfaction.'

'You don't find me attractive?' Kirsty rummaged for her comb in the depths of her bag, determined not to look a mess.

'On the contrary. I find you most attractive.' He made no move towards her. 'This is part of the trouble. I should keep away from you for your own good, but am finding it difficult.'

'You could try asking me what I want.' She was furious at his assumption that it was all down to him.

'And what is that?' His very calm added fuel to her fire.

'I would like to get to know you.' She was not being truthful, unable to say that she wanted to become part of his life, to share everything, including his bed, to have his children and never, never part.

'Kirsty, I can't risk you falling in love with me.' He said this simply, without a trace of arrogance. 'It is best if we don't meet again. I'll take you back to the Hall and Barend will drive you home.'

'I have no home. Thanks to that rat of a boyfriend. Are all you men the same? Selfish, cruel, unfaithful bastards?' She followed him from the vault, seething with anger, her clothing chaffing the welts the whip had inflicted.

'Not all. One day perhaps you will understand why I've acted like this. Maybe it's the most unselfish thing I've ever done.'

Barend was waiting, once more attired in uniform, the limousine parked at the bottom of the steps.

Kirsty flung her wrap around her shoulders, turned her back on Dirk and went down. Barend opened the rear door for her.

Dirk called out, 'Goodbye, Kirsty.'

She didn't bother to reply.

'Well, I don't know what to say, darling. Aren't you the lucky one with three guys after you? So, what's the problem? Why aren't you dancing with joy?'

Gina had pulled up outside Tregaskis Cottage half an hour before. She intended to stay for a week, having left Kelly in control of the business. Craig had sulked because she refused to take him along, but she wanted to be free to play the field and sample the Cornishmen. Now, having toured the cottage and stashed her luggage, he was drinking coffee in the kitchen and feeling her way into Kirsty's emotional state. What she had discovered so far was not reassuring.

'It's hard to explain.' Kirsty went to fetch the biscuits. Gina got the impression that she was finding it hard to express herself. This was unusual. 'There's been so much to do. I haven't got this place straight yet. There're still boxes to unpack, and as for the shop! I'm looking for an Andy replacement.'

'He's doing OK. I've been around to see him. Domestic bliss with him and Alec. It's quite beautiful. Restores one's faith in human beings.'

'I guess it does.' Kirsty sounded distracted.

Gina knew what hard work moving entailed, but even so she felt there was more behind her friend's strange mood. She put down her cup, stared straight at her and said, 'Come on, girl. Tell your old Auntie Gina all about it.'

Kirsty pushed her hands through her hair. It was streaky blonde now. She'd been lying in the sun and this had bleached it. She seemed reluctant to speak, and when she did, she was hesitant.

'It's this man... Dirk Stratten.'

'You've mentioned him. What's wrong? Is he gay or something?' Gina lit a cigarette. She was struggling to give them up but sometimes indulged.

Kirsty took to a restless pacing. 'No, not gay, but he's a mystery. He invited me to go to his house one evening. That's it, over there,' and she pointed in the direction of the headland.

Gina went across and looked out of the window. 'Can't see a thing.'

'You'd have to stand closer to the cliffs. Anyhow, it's called Rosewood Manor and is as ancient as the hills.'

'And he isn't, I take it? Young and virile.'

'It seems so, and yet there's a depth of wisdom and knowledge about him that's aeons old.'

'He's rich and well-travelled. That might account for it. Had an expensive education, went to Oxford or Cambridge, maybe?'

'It's more than that.' Kirsty seemed genuinely upset. 'And he's into S&M. He chained me and then whipped me."

'Ah, I see.' Warning bells clanged in Gina's brain. The trouble with Kirsty was that she always got deeply involved with men who were complicated. A simple, straightforward guy didn't turn her on.

'I'd like to meet him. Find out where he's at.' Gina had always acted as a kind of barometer when it came to Kirsty's attachments, because she didn't always listen to her inner promptings. Witness Martin.

'I don't think that'll be possible. He's not out and about much and seems to have dropped me like a brick.'

'You can introduce me to Robert and Seth. They sound pretty regular guys.'

'We'll go to *The Pig and Firkin*. That's where I stayed while house hunting.'

Gina was convinced that Kirsty was hiding something. 'Whatever you say, but tell me more about Dirk. He sounds intriguing.'

'That's the trouble. He is very intriguing.'

'Has he fucked you?'

Kirsty stopped in front of her, hands on hips, eyes blazing. 'He's fucked with my head!'

'How so?'

Kirsty straddled a tall stool, exasperated. 'He was sweetness itself, to begin with. We had dinner and he took me round the house. Then he opened a secret passage and we went down into the vault. It was filled with the most fabulous treasure. He draped me in jewels. I didn't want them. They made me feel uncomfortable. We went into another underground room. It was kitted out with whips and things...'

The very mention of this was enough to make Gina's pussy spasm. No stranger to such perverse pleasures, she wanted to hear more. 'Go on. What happened next?'

'We talked and then he blind-folded and stripped me and chained me to a crosspiece.'

Gina could not sit still, her nipples crimping and her clitoris swelling as she imagined Kirsty bound naked to the whipping post. 'And then?' she urged.

Kirsty rested her elbows on the table and bowed her head in her hands. 'Then he spanked me.'

'With his hand?'

'Yes, it hurt and it was horrible. Martin used to do this sometimes and I came to enjoy it, but this man is a stranger and I've never been so humiliated.'

'I'll bet.' Even as she said this, Gina was thinking, I must meet this big brute!

'He took a whip to me, thrashed me and then turned me to face him, took off my restraints, kissed and fondled me and then started to frig me. I was on the point of climax when he got out his cock and put it in me. He lifted me and sat me on it, went in and out a few times and then left me stranded. I was on the point of coming, so bloody frustrated. He told me that he didn't want to have me fall in love with him. It would be dangerous if I did.'

'Has he a jealous wife?'

Kirsty shook her head. 'No. Nor partners or children or family.'

'How odd. I shall investigate, never fear. We'll find out what's behind all this.'

'I dressed and Barend, that's his butler person, drove me home. I've not seen or heard from Dirk since.'

'You're not going to leave it like that, are you?'

Kirsty sighed. 'I'm tired, Gina. It's been one hell of a haul, setting up house and the shop, too. Robert's been great, but whenever I start thinking about getting close to him something happens to prevent it. It was the same with Seth. We were on the point of making it when he was nearly concussed by a flying stone.'

'Looks like someone's out to get you.' Gina was joking and yet began to wonder. She changed the subject. 'OK. Let's get on something sexy and wow the local yokels.'

Chapter Five

'What's bugging you, my friend? Have you lost your nerve? Or perhaps you wish to stay as you are, the eternal wanderer? Not a bad choice, I may say. Boundless health, no aging, no illness and no death. I did you a good turn, Dirk, and that wishy-washy Angel Gabriel stood no chance. I ask you, where are you going to find a woman prepared to give her life for you?' Lucian observed as he lounged on the bed of the Master Chamber, buffing his nails.

He was wearing a white silk suit, draped and loose fitting, the very height of fashion. Dirk knew that he never stinted himself when it came to personal adornment or anything else for that matter. He also recognised that Lucian was taking delight in rubbing salt into his wounds. Dirk wasn't blind to the fact that it was in his interest to maintain the status quo. Every statistic counted in his favour and he didn't intend to lose his hold.

Kirsty's departure had hurt Dirk more than he cared to admit. He had recognised a soul mate in her, hoping against all hope that she'd be willing to join and save him, but at the same time praying that she would refuse. In that moment he had loved another being more than himself and was struggling to keep it that way. Lucian didn't make it any easier with his constant carping.

It had been a lengthy association, immensely profitable in material ways, but Dirk often bitterly recalled the saying, 'Who sups with the devil needs a long spoon.'

Intelligent and clever, he was no match for Lucian. One major advantage, or maybe disadvantage, was his ability to love, even now after decades of despair. Lucian would never love, his emotions burned to a crisp during the War in Heaven, when he had lost the battle and been cast out. He had recounted this story to Dirk over and over, in danger of becoming a *Paradise Lost* bore.

'So, she's given up on you, eh?' Lucian uncoiled his limbs and rose to his full, impressive height. 'I'd have imagined you'd do better than that. Are you losing your touch, old chap?'

'Why don't you go back to Hell?' Sometimes Lucian tried Dirk's patience beyond endurance.

'I'm having too much fun here. Did you know that Kirsty has a friend staying? A lovely piece of arse called Gina. I've delved into her background and she enjoys having different partners, not necessarily male, and loves sex games. She'd adore the vault.'

Dirk's interest sharpened at the mention of Kirsty, yet he was angry with himself for acting like a lovesick schoolboy. He was considering leaving this peaceful stretch of coast and taking himself off to some wilder clime. To do this, he needed Lucian's cooperation and he seemed determined that they should remain there longer. It was almost as if he knew something that Dirk didn't and was working to a hidden agenda.

'Leave her alone and Kirsty, too.' He stood by the upper window, staring at the distant panorama of glittering sea where the waves were crowned with foaming white horses. It was incredibly beautiful and he had never lost his appreciation of wonderful scenery.

His heart ached with longing to be human again, living a simple life with a wife and children and the expectancy of a peaceful death at the end. Surely, what he had done was not so wicked as to deserve such a punishment? Hubris, his ungovernable pride had been his downfall. He was struggling to control this even now and the first step was to deny himself Kirsty.

'Look, my friend, look. Here are the two of them, Gina and Kirsty, hot for love.' Lucian indicated the wall mirror. 'I wonder if they'll give into the temptation to rub each other's clits and finger their holes.'

Dirk couldn't help staring at the images of Kirsty and the redhead who was with her. They were in a bedroom, half naked as they tried on this garment or that, laughing and joking, yet he sensed that Kirsty was troubled. 'We shouldn't be spying on them. This is the wrong use of magic.'

'Oh, don't be so prissy! What's the point of having special powers if one can't play with them? I'd fuck either girl. Both together, perhaps. Cunts and mouths and arseholes. What d'you say?'

Despite himself, lust thickened Dirk's cock as he listened to those seductive words. It was only Kirsty he wanted, but the other could keep Lucian occupied. His good resolutions began to waver. 'I'm not sure.'

'Excellent. That means you're up for it. They're heading for *The Pig and Firkin*. We'll arrive there casually and see how the land lies. Meanwhile, I'm going I visit Aphrodite and find out what's new.' Lucian clicked his fingers and vanished from Dirk's sight.

'He'll do me,' Gina said, as she sashayed into the public bar and clapped eyes on Seth. 'Is that him, Kirsty? The surfing guy? Get him over here.'

Kirsty felt her depression lifting in Gina's company. They found a table and sat down. She had no need to beckon Seth. He was there in an instant. 'Hello, long time no see. Are you sorted, Kirsty? Getting everything ship-shape?' As he talked, he was eyeing Gina who had adopted one of her most fetching poses. Her short denim skirt rose higher as she crossed her legs and leaned forward to deepen her cleavage.

'I'm getting there. The shop opens on Monday and the cottage is beginning to look like home. Thank you for recommending your decorator buddies. They've been more than just helpful. This is Gina. She's staying with me for a few days. Gina, meet Seth.'

Now I may as well make myself scarce, Kirsty thought. Gina has that glint in her eye. Seth wont be sleeping alone tonight.

The fact that he could be so fickle didn't bother her. Robert rang her almost every day and she had arranged to meet him later, but even this left her cold. It wasn't him she wanted, or Seth. Trying to be sensible, she realised that Dirk's indifference was making her even hotter for him.

Gina's policy was, 'Treat 'em mean, keep 'em keen.' Kirsty found it hard to be that tough, but it was apparent that Dirk could do it.

Seth bought them drinks, cider for Gina who wanted to taste the brew made from local apples, and gin and tonic for Kirsty. They were joined by the surfing brotherhood. It was the height of the season and rivalries ran strong. Strangers had come, issuing challenges, Australians, New Zealanders, and Californians. The reputation of the North Cornwall waves was worldwide. Gina was in her element surrounded by this bunch of outdoor men.

They were muscular and deeply tanned from exposure to the sun, winds and salt water that had also bleached their hair. They wore necklaces made of small colourful beads, the mark of a true surfer. Kirsty sat there unmoved. She wished it were otherwise, regretting ever meeting Dirk Stratten. It wasn't much better when Robert walked in and she introduced him to Gina.

'He's fit!' was Gina's whispered observation. 'No wonder you opted for this place. It's bursting with talent!' And she went back to flirting with Seth.

'Is she with you for long?' Robert sat beside Kirsty, his arm resting along the back of the bench.

'A few days. She likes it here and may be looking for a shop. Can you advise her?'

'Certainly, but it won't be quite the same. You're special, Kirsty, but you've been rather distant lately. No pressure, but have I offended in some way?' His eyes were clear and candid and there was nothing mysterious about him. She rather wished there was, for this might make him more fascinating. What you saw was what you got with Robert.

'Not at all. It's me, if anything. I've been so reoccupied with moving.'

'I understand.' He pressed her hand and her fingers relaxed in his. He was such a nice person and would make an excellent husband and father.

Then why didn't the prospect thrill her? Robert could kiss and caress her and her blood scarcely warmed, whereas the merest touch of Dirk's little finger had her to the point of explosion.

She tested her reactions, just to be sure, moving closer to him until her thigh was against his. She felt the returning pressure and his hand closed on hers, his other arm leaving the seat back and coming to rest on her shoulders. It was reassuring and comfortable, but didn't cause mayhem with her hormones, light a fire in her loins or make her clit throb. All these things happened without warning when she glanced across the room and saw Dirk.

She hadn't seen him enter, but there he was at a table with Lucian and three lovely women. One was a big-breasted blonde wearing a flimsy dress that revealed more than it concealed. The other two appeared to be identical twins, dressed in hipster jeans and brief tops, dark-eyed, dark-haired and Oriental looking.

It was a shock. Kirsty couldn't speak, but Robert said, 'There's Mr Stratten and friends. I haven't noticed him in here before. Shouldn't have thought it his kind of place.'

She heartily wished that he wasn't there now, but brushed it aside as of little interest. In reality, she couldn't stop looking at him. Lucian caught her eye and raised his glass in her direction, nodding mockingly. She bit her lip and turned away, but had seen enough. The blonde was all over Lucian, while he appeared to be disinterested. The twins were seated either side of Dirk, arms around his neck and bodies pressed close to his, looking at him adoringly.

Kirsty wanted to point him out to Gina, but she was surrounded by surfers. Suddenly Kirsty began to panic. She had to get out of there. Gina knew her way back to the cottage and could get a cab.

'Shall we go, Robert? What about a visit to *The Admiral s Arms?*' she suggested.

'But Gina...? It would be impolite to abandon her.'

'I'm sure she can cope.' The urge to get up and go was becoming even more pressing. Kirsty half rose then winced, pain shooting through her ankle and forcing her down again.

'What is it?' Robert was all concern.

'I don't know. A really bad pain that starts when I try to stand.' She rubbed her hand up and down her leg and the agony abated.

'A sprain, I expect. Have you been overdoing it? Lifting too heavy objects? I advised that you wait until I could help you. Why didn't you listen?' He scolded her like a father and this made her impatient. She'd learned her lesson with Martin and vowed that he was the last man she would ever allow to boss her around.

'I managed very well and no, I haven't hurt myself. Don't fuss, Robert. I'll just sit here until it feels better.'

'Can I get you another drink?'

She nodded. 'Thank you, but make it orange juice. I'm driving.' She felt mean for being short with him. He was always so kind.

It was crowded at the bar and she was glad of the respite from his company. She stared across at Dirk and he looked up.

The bar melted away. Dirk took her hands in his and they both drifted higher and higher. The ceiling and roof dissolved and they were floating above the port and following the silver path of moonlight across the sea. The cliffs lay below them and Kirsty was wrapped tightly in Dirk's arms. She wasn't afraid, clinging to him, lifting her mouth to his and being absorbed in his kiss. His hands cupped her breasts as gently as if she was made of spun glass and he raised her until she lay across his rms. His lips travelled down her body and her clothing dissolved. Next she felt his mouth on her delta, parting the lips and licking her clitoris.

She imagined that she cried out as her climax pierced her, thought that she was falling, then found that she hadn't left the bench and Robert was standing by her and placing a glass on the table. Dirk no longer looked her way, but he seemed to have withdrawn, ignoring the girls, gazing into space. Lucian, however, fixed her with his feral eyes, even while he boldly fondled the blonde. Icy shocks ran through Kirsty. He knew where he and Dirk had just been, had watched them in that uncanny space between reality and the dream world. How could this be?

'Are you OK?' Gina bent over her. 'You look as if you've seen a ghost.'

'I'm fine. It's nothing. I may have sprained my ankle, that's all. Robert's looking after me.' Kirsty wished he wasn't, wanting to tell Gina that Dirk was there. She thought up that age old excuse. 'I'm going to the little girls' room, Robert. Shan't be a minute.'

'Me, too.' Gina caught on and they went off together. Kirsty's foot was fine now, without a hint of pain.

The pink and white, rather old-fashioned cloakroom was empty. Big cabbage roses sprawled over the wallpaper and there were mirrors in gilt frames. It was spotlessly clean and smelled of lavender.

'He's here, Gina.'

'Who?' Gina leaned closer to one of the mirrors and added a touch more mascara to her lashes.

'Dirk Stratten.'

'Ah, that's why you're all flustered. Is he that handsome hunk sitting with a fair-haired guy, a busty blonde and two chicks?'

'Yes, that's him. Now can you see what I mean about him?'

'I guess, though he seems full of himself. Robert is much nicer, I imagine.'

'You should know that nice doesn't necessarily mean sexy.' Kirsty was finding it hard to explain the turmoil within her, the ache in her pussy, and the tingle in her nipples that the very mention of Dirk evoked. She was wet, too, almost as if she really had climaxed. She tried to explain to Gina. 'I felt that I was with him just now... not here, but floating through the night sky.'

Gina gave her a sharp stare. 'Hell, what are you on? It sounds pretty pokey gear to me.'

'Nothing. No drugs and I've only had one drink. I was with him, I tell you, and he was kissing me and then sucking my clit. I came violently.' To talk of it sent shivers through Kirsty and made her long for him.

Gina paused in making herself even more stunning and her concerned eyes met Kirsty's in the mirror. 'Darling, I think you've been living alone too long. Get out more. Date Robert and Seth and stop mooning over Dirk. Haven't you made any girlfriends here that you can go on the pull with?'

'No, and this isn't a city, you know. It's a rather staid fishing port and girls don't go out "on the pull", as you crudely put it.'

'Ha, sorry I spoke! But I'm worried about you. This is all in your imagination, you know. You didn't really go space walking with Dirk and have celestial sex.'

'Prove it.' Kirsty was desperately clinging to the reality the experience.

'You prove that it happened.'

'I can't.'

'There you are then. I suggest that we tackle Dirk about it, ask him outright if he brought you off in the sky.'

Kirsty could feel heat flushing all over her. 'I couldn't do that!'

'Why not? I will if you won't. Come on.'

Dirk could hardly believe that it had been so easy to transport Kirsty through space. No one had been aware at they had gone. Time had stopped fractionally. He had held her, kissed her, brought her to the peak of sensation and then they were back in the pub. They had never really left. This was magic used for the best possible purpose - to help love blossom, but at the same time he was afraid that it might go too far. Kirsty's welfare was still his main concern, but she was so very tempting.

He cursed Lucian for putting him in this unenviable position and, for once, was totally unsure of himself. He had tried to contact Gabriel for advice, but that angel, more female than male, had been busy bearing news of conception to mothers or helping those going through the agony of childbirth. This was his/her special department.

'You're on your own, old chap.' Dirk caught Lucian's eye and heard his words ringing in his brain.

The twins were doing their best to arouse him, but they meant nothing. He saw Kirsty and her companion leaving the restroom and come towards him. He was on guard trying to squash the hopes and fears raging within him.

Kirsty paused near the bar and he heard the landlord say, 'Mr Caldecote has left, Miss Anderson. He was feeling unwell and asked me to pass the message on.'

This came as no surprise to Dirk. He had cast a sickness spell on Robert and made Kirsty's ankle hurt in the same way that he had summoned up a storm for her first visit to the estate agent's home, though it was Lucian who had hit Seth with a pebble. Despite his doubts and misgivings, Dirk couldn't tolerate the idea of her fucking any other man. Now the field was clear, and he was confused, wishing to protect her from harm, but unable to do without her.

He rose from his chair and bowed as Kirsty presented Gina. 'Charmed, I'm sure.' Reading her mind, he caught a strong sense of distrust, suspicion and the determination to protect Kirsty. This was a formidable friend and he must win her over.

Lucian came to his aid, without bothering to stand, one hand buried in the blonde's lap. 'I've always admired red hair and yours is natural. No doubt your bush is the same colour.' He gave Gina the full benefit of his knowing smile and blazing yellowish eyes.

'You're right.'

She was brash and confident. Dirk knew that she would fight to the death for Kirsty. Lucian had rightly said that she experimented with sex, enjoyed domination and submission, but her loyalty to her friend was her mainstay. If she discovered that Dirk had the power to demand her love, then she would become his enemy, opposing him with all her might. He wanted to tell her, to beg her to stop him, but the crying need in his soul was too strong.

'I was under the impression that you never wanted to see me again,' he heard Kirsty say. 'So what was all that about just now? You know what took place. Don't bother to deny it.'

He didn't, neither did he speak aloud. There was no need. Her spirit could hear him. 'I couldn't stop myself. Oh, Kirsty, if only you knew how much I've longed for you.' He was holding her pressed close to his heart, but no onlooker was aware.

'Tell me what troubles you,' she begged, arms tight about him.

'Not yet. I can't bear to lose you.'

Lucian's voice was like a thunderclap, smashing through the veil and dragging them back to their bodies. 'Let's have a party. What about it, Dirk? Shall they visit Rosewood?'

'Would you like that?' Dirk saw Kirsty's bewilderment.

'I don't know. What do you want to do, Gina?'

'Is Seth invited?'

Lucian answered for him. 'Yes, and the surfers. We'll start at Rough Tor. There are sure to be fairies about on such a night as this. Meet Aphrodite and her babes. They'll ensure everyone has a good time.'

Dirk guessed that Lucian was up to mischief, but didn't have the will to stop him. All he could see was Kirsty and all he could feel was the uncontrollable desire to have her with him.

'Rough Tor has been avoided for generations by those who live in the area,' pronounced Seth. 'It has a bad reputation for being a meeting place for the devil and his witches. Archaeologists said it was a rock swept down from the north by a glacier during the ice-age. The Cornish folk won't have this. They know best. It's the work of Old Scratch, the local name for Satan.'

Kirsty and Gina listened and nodded. Kirsty hadn't visited it before, though reading about it in guide books. It had never occurred to her that she might go there with Dirk.

They had left the inn and Kirsty drove her own car with Gina and Seth. He was the only surfer who had elected to go. They seemed suspicious of Dirk and Lucian, despite the allure of their female companions. Barend had been waiting to chauffeur his boss. The road wound up towards the moor. It was deserted and Kirsty was already regretting agreeing to take part. She was sober and clinging to rationality, trying to ignore Gina and Seth who were in a passionate clinch on the back seat.

The moor stretched before her, bathed in moonlight, ghostly and mysterious.

Gina broke from Seth's kiss to say, 'It's like *The Hound Of The Baskerville.*'

He silenced her mouth with his.

Glancing in the rear mirror, Kirsty could see the limousine. It overtook her and she followed as it headed for the huge black shape looming ahead. It seemed to be advancing, a sinister figure seeking her. Closer up revealed that it was a slab of grey granite, twenty feet tall, thrusting upwards like a warning finger. It had been there for aeons, a standing stone positioned by nature as a solitary sentinel. Tribes had come and gone, the world had been torn apart by war, floods and disasters yet this immovable monolith had remained. There was something remorseless about it.

The limousine purred to a stop and its passengers jumped out. Aphrodite began to sway and chant, worshipping the stone. The twins joined her, stripping off their clothes, their lithe bodies gleaming. Barend stood by the car, motionless as a statue carved from ivory. Lucian treated the relic with contempt, as if denying that it had any special powers. Dirk came over to Kirsty as she was leaving the driver's seat, took her hands in his and hurried her to the opposite side where the monument cast a dense shadow.

She had no time to see if Gina was all right, whirled into a situation that gave no credence to common sense. All that mattered was Dirk's mouth capturing hers and is hands familiarising themselves with her every curve and contour. He pressed her against the stone, its age-old chill penetrating her spine. He murmured as he caressed her, using an unfamiliar language, but she caught the drift of his words - he wanted her, needed her. Was it possible that he loved her?

She had the eerie feeling that the stone was watching them. Its brooding presence was unseen but dominating, like a sleeping dragon coiled beneath the earth. A shiver ran through her.

'What is it?' He held her even tighter.

'This place. It's evil.'

'And private. We could make love here and no one would see us.' His hands had raised her crop-top, found their way into her bra and cupped the fullness there. Oh, you have such beautiful breasts,' he muttered, and lowered his head to suck each in turn.

Sensations fired through her body as his tongue rasped over her nipples. Suddenly the monolith became a friend, supporting her as he lifted her skirt and pushed aside her panties. He found her clit and she came in a rush, shuddering with the intensity of an orgasm that had been triggered by a single touch. She was amazed at her response. Even as the ripples faded, she was eager to have his cock inside her.

He pulled away, but she clung to him. She could see his eyes and teeth gleaming against the darkness. 'You want more?'

She was like a creature possessed. 'Yes! Yes!'

'You want to feel me inside you, making you a part of me, flesh of my flesh, bone of my bone?'

'Please. Stop torturing me.'

His hands were on her shoulders, forcing her to her knees in front of him. The grass was damp, penetrating her skirt, but she was hardly aware, watching as he unzipped his fly, setting his erection free. Her hand came up and folded round it, feeling the exquisite smoothness of the stem and the pre-come seeping from the helm. It was too dark to see it properly, but she could guess its length and girth, a formidable weapon. She wanted to take it into her, filling her to capacity, butting against her womb and giving her muscles something to clench around.

He sighed deeply, head thrown back, eyes half closed. 'Your touch is divine.'

Encouraged, she increased her movements, drawing the foreskin up over the glans and then easing it down again. 'Take me,' she pleaded.

'Not yet. Use your lips on me.'

She leaned closer, opened her mouth and eased his cock-head in, stretching widely to accommodate it. He pushed, holding her by the hair, seeking that all-embracing pleasure. He stood firmly, legs slightly apart as he braced himself. She was engulfed in the fragrance of him, clean linen and shower gel, the musky odour of aroused male, trapped in his pubic hair. She took him, inch by inch, half fearing that she would choke on the size. His hand fastened around the base of his cock, testing how far he could go. She caressed its length with her tongue, wanted to give him the ecstasy he had just lavished on her.

Despite his strength, he was amazingly considerate. He didn't force his penis into her mouth, jab at her throat and make her choke. If this act could be called gentlemanly, then he was the perfect gentleman. But gradually he began to lose control. He penetrated her again, thrusting this time, his teeth clenched as he panted. He drew out, then slid in and she closed her throat muscles, trying to clench around him and give him the greatest sensation.

In and out he rode her, passion getting the better of him. Harder now, and her lips felt bruised but she was loving it, one hand inside his pants, cupping the heavy balls. She wished she could do it where she could see him, wanted to read the expression contorting his face as he neared crisis point. His hips were jutting against her as he powered his cock, in and out, faster and faster.

'I'm coming...' he growled. 'Take all of it, Kirsty. Take all of me.'

His cock jerked and she felt the first rush of semen filling her mouth. More followed, entering her throat and spilling around her lips in a hot deluge. She wallowed, glad to drink in this tribute. Delight swamped her along with his fluid. Now, surely, he would enter her, mark her as his own forever?

She rose from her knees, reached up and wrapped her arms round his neck, whispering, 'Take me, Dirk.'

'Maybe I will... in time. But as I said before, you mustn't become too attached to me, and certainly don't all in love.'

It was like the blast from a cold water jet. Her heart plummeted and her fires died abruptly. 'Why? What have I done?'

'Nothing. You are perfect. That's part of the trouble.' He sounded so sad that she wanted to cradle his head in her arms and kiss him better. 'Then what is it? You owe me an explanation.'

'Be patient. I'll tell you if and when the time is right.'

Lucian interrupted them, sticking his head round the monolith. 'Have you two finished? Let's get going. Back to the manor and on with the show.'

It was the strangest party Gina had ever attended, and she'd been to many. Not only was it highly erotic, but the crowd were beyond belief. She accepted that swingers often liked to dress up, wear masks, be other than what they were in daily life, but this was extreme! How had timid little Kirsty got herself mixed up with such a crowd?

Seth, though pretending to be a man of the world, was obviously shocked though aroused. She guessed that nothing like this had impinged on his simple life and this amused her.

'Time to stop being a country bumpkin, Seth, my lad,' she chided, when his eyes widened as he watched Aphrodite pole-dancing in front of a crowd of men sporting large erections.

'Where did all these weirdoes come from?' He was swaying slightly, having imbibed heavily of Dirk's free alcohol. Gina had serious doubts about his stamina. He'd probably develop 'brewer's droop' and be unable to perform.

'I haven't a clue, guess they're Dirk's pals.'

She had to agree that they were unusual. A motley selection of men ranging from handsome, muscular body-builders to transvestites, elegant in expensive dresses. The female element were as varied. A leather clad dominatrix strode around flourishing a whip. Gorgeous model girls paraded their beauty. Hookers touted for business. Sexual encounters were taking place in every room, landing and staircase and spilling over on to the terraces.

The most varied action was in the vault. Gina didn't hesitate to go down there, accustomed to similar scenes among the circle in which she moved. Lucian intrigued her and she wanted to know him better. There was no doubt that he was a bad boy and these were always appealing. She wanted to pit her sexual prowess against his and give that blonde bimbo something to think about. Aphrodite, she called herself. The Goddess of love? Gina thought, we'll see about at! She may lose her crown by the end of the night.

'Where do these people come from?' Kirsty stayed close to Dirk as they entered the reception room. It was dominated by a large television screen where a pair of porn stars cavorted on film, their cries and moans rising above the general hubbub of talk, laughter and propositioning on all sides.

He shrugged. 'Lucian has the knack of getting what he wants at the snap of his fingers. You think these are mortal? Imagine them to be made of bone, flesh and blood? Can you tell what is real and what illusion?'

'I don't understand.'

'You don't have to. We'll go away somewhere quiet, shall we?'

He passed a hand over her eyes and they were in his bedroom. A fire crackled in the hearth as she had imagined it the first time. The air was fragrant with patchouli oil. Music drifted from concealed speakers. She recognized one of her favourite composers. The setting couldn't have been more perfect. She sank into a deeply cushioned couch and Dirk paced the room restlessly and began to speak.

It was like an adventure story. He told her of his boyhood in the Netherlands and how he had gone to sea. He spoke of many lands as if they were newly discovered by him, and she knew that they had been established on maps for centuries. His tales became stranger, transporting her to foreign oceans where tempests roared and the waves were high as mountains. She wondered if he was drunk. Though his eyes shone fanatically, his speech wasn't slurred and he seemed in control. Why was it, then, that he related these things as if they were facts that he had observed with his own eyes? They covered hundreds of years.

She interrupted him at one point. 'Are you an historian?'

He gave a harsh laugh. 'You could call me that, I suppose.'

The firelight shone on his face, rendering it demonic, and fear engulfed her. Over and above that she felt overwhelming love. Dirk had captured her, body and soul, but there were so many unanswered questions.

He paused by her chair and drew her to her feet and she slid her arms around his body and rested her head on his chest. Peace engulfed her. They were alone. There was no one to interrupt them. Whatever happened in the future, just for that little space in time, they belonged to one another.

'Dirk, Dirk... I've waited so long for you.'

'And I for you, darling.'

He lifted her and carried her to the bed. After laying her down he started to remove her clothing. It didn't take long and soon she was bare and he devoured her with hot eyes. No longer the tender lover, he tore his pants open and entered her in one savage thrust.

She felt that she had been there before, done this before, but on the astral plane. This was real. He was *real*. Made up of flesh, blood and muscle. He took her violently, driven by need and she gloried in it. She was crushed against the mattress as he drove into her with ravaging intensity. He hauled her to her knees and took her from behind, his hand reaching round to rub her clit. Ecstasy swept through her as he stroked her roughly. She pushed her hips against him at every inward stroke of his penis penetrating her. They rent the air with their savage cries, coupled with the wet sound of his wild invasion of her body. She screamed as a mighty orgasm tore through her, tossing her high and plunging her down. He rolled her over and mounted her again. She felt his spunk filling her and beat at his back with her fists and clawed at his skin.

He braced himself on his arms and stared at her so hard that she felt she was drowning in his sea-green yes. With a long drawn sigh he sank down, resting his head on her shoulder. Kirsty closed her eyes and held him fast in her arms. This was bliss and she was sure it would last forever.

Then he stirred, rose up again and said, 'Never forget that you mustn't love me.'

Chapter Six

Dirk walked Kirsty home at dawn. They took a shortcut along the cliff.

The first rays of morning fanned down from a sky that was rainbow-coloured in the east and shrouded by night-clouds westward. It was that awesome moment when the world seems poised. Would there be another day? Or would some cataclysm hurl mankind into the abyss? He had witnessed so many dawns and each one had held this second of dread, but nothing happened. There was no sounding of the Last Trump.

Kirsty was beside him, but refused to take his arm.

He knew he had hurt her by insisting that there was to be no permanence in their relationship, yet this was the only way he could save her. The party had quietened, the participants exhausted by over-indulgence in sexual activities. Soon they would be banished to their own regions - human, inhuman, they would obey.

'Thank you,' Kirsty said stiffly when they reached the gate of Tregaskis Cottage. 'There's no need to come any further.'

The pain in her eyes was unbearable. He spread his hands wide in a helpless gesture. 'It's for your own good, Kirsty.'

'You didn't say that when you were fucking me.'

It was on the tip of his tongue to retort, 'I'm only human,' then remembered that he wasn't. All he could reply was, 'Sorry.'

'Don't worry about it. That's how it is these days... casual sex that means little or nothing... no more important than a handshake.' She lifted the latch and stepped through the gate, closing it behind her. 'Will you see that Gina gets back safely? She's not familiar with the layout yet.'

'Barend will bring her.'

'Thank you.' She was being so formal, hardly recognizable from the girl who had climaxed in his arms.

The sun was rising fast, driving away the mists, promising another warm day. Dirk watched Kirsty go up the path and let herself in through the front door. Then he turned away.

'What a wacky crew!' Seth got out of the limousine after Gina.

'You can say that again!' she agreed as he let her into his shop and took her to the living area. 'I didn't expect anything like it in this quiet backwater.'

'I thought you'd screw the lot!' He grinned at her as he switched on the kettle, found the jar of instant coffee, sugar and a couple of mugs. 'That Aphrodite bird... a right tart! God, she likes to spread it about.'

'You could have had her. Didn't you fancy it?' Gina flopped down on the settee, so tired she could hardly keep her eyes open.

'It was you I wanted, honey, and still do.' He parked himself beside her.

'Bet you say that to all the girls. You had me, anyhow.'

'And I want to do it again. Why d'you think I brought you home with me?'

'I'm pretty bushed. Can I have a nap first?'

'I'm glad you said that. Come on, let's go upstairs.

'What did you make of Dirk Stratten's mates?'

'Were they his or that vampire type Lucian's? He's devastatingly good-looking, but gives me the creeps. I wonder if he'd be an outstanding screw?'

'You could have tried him.' Seth led the way to his loft bedroom.

Gina followed, yawning widely. The party, orgy or whatever had been intensely stimulating, but she stuck with Seth, wary of the others. She had noticed that Kirsty had disappeared with Dirk and hoped it had gone well. For her part, she wanted to pursue her investigation of Seth, his parts, intentions and general attitude to life. So far he was great, and she stripped, threw back the duvet and snuggled into his bed. He joined her, frigged and fucked her and she fell asleep at last, well satisfied with her Cornishman.

Lucian had banished his guests at the first hint of birdsong that heralded the day. He had heard Dirk and needed to have a talk with him. With his capacity for diving into the minds and thoughts of all and sundry, he was disturbed by what he had observed passing between him and Kirsty.

His wily brain had come up with another idea. Why not kill two birds with one stone? It would be even better if he could capture her soul as well as Dirk's. Yet even he had boundaries. There was no such thing as free will. Aphrodite was annoyed with him for not paying her enough attention and had returned to her club, dragging the twins along, too. Lucian was too old and wise to take any notice. He had other fish to fry.

Dirk was in a sullen mood when he came in. He wanted to disappear to his room, but Lucian stopped him. 'So you've shagged her. Was it worth it?'

Dirk went to pass him in the conservatory, but Lucian, taking his ease in a basket chair, stuck out a leg and stopped him. He looked up with his slanting feline eyes and Dirk said, 'It was well worth it, if you must know.'

'You're falling for her. It won't do. You'll only be let down again.'

'So be it. I'll be condemned to wandering.'

'Have you forgotten what it's like? You need a reminder.'

The light faded. The glass roof vanished, so did Rosewood. They stood on a heaving deck, waves crashing around them and a hurricane in full blast. The sails billowed and flapped. Some had been torn from the rigging. Dirk clung to the wheel, but there was no way he could control the vessel. He glimpsed the crew struggling to batten down hatches and lash ropes in place. They were thin and haggard, more like corpses than living men. The seas were monumental, the ship pitching and tossing like a cork. Thunder clouds scudded across the sky. Lightning flashed. All hell was let lose and Lucian was in the crow's nest at the top of the mainmast, roaring with laughter.

'You really want this, Dirk?' he shouted in Dirk's brain.

'Better by far than condemning her.'

'Bugger you, then.' The conservatory surrounded Dirk gain, filled with sunshine and the scent of rare plants. Lucian had gone from sight, but he whispered, 'Next time I see her, I'll ask what she would be prepared to do for you.'

'Stay out of it!'
'My dear boy, it's more than my job's worth!'

Opening day. Kirsty was up bright and early. Meg had become a part-time assistant to supplement her pub wages and Gina had offered to help.

The shop looked great. Kirsty had filled it with some of her best pieces and used drapes designed by Gina. Brass glinted, furniture gleamed. There were oil paintings in elaborate frames, Victorian workboxes, a doll's house from the same period, plus a French cradle draped in white lace, circa eighteen-sixty. Vases in pairs, crystal dressing table sets, fencing foils, walking-sticks, dinner services and silver coffee pots, small items of jewellery, hat pins and feather boas. Nothing was less than ninety years old.

She was more than satisfied. The shop was well stocked. There were packing cases still to be gone through and then she would venture to auction sales. She had a warm feeling within telling her that she was going to be successful. She forgot Dirk temporarily.

Nine o'clock and Robert was the first customer. He seemed pleased to find Kirsty alone. 'It looks great, very classy.'

'Thank you. I think it's even better than the Bath shop. The building lends itself to it. Would you like a cup of coffee? We're giving one to customers today as a gesture of good will.'

He nodded and she went to a magnificent Edwardian sideboard where cups stood on a tray and an electric kettle had already boiled. 'I've seen your adverts in the Newquay Guardian and the Lanyon Bray Gazette. You shouldn't find it hard to drum up trade.'

'Is there anything here that interests you?' She stood beside him, coffee cup in hand, keeping an eye on the window where passers-by were pausing to stare.

'I'm trying to find a present for my mother. She's seventy next week.'

'Have you any idea what she might like?' It was better to get down to business than cope with the uncomfortable feeling that he wanted more from her than she was prepared to give. It might have been possible had she not met Dirk.

'I've thought about a brooch,' he replied.

She unlocked the glass-fronted cabinet and lifted out a tray of gems. He settled on a bow-shaped one studded with paste diamonds. 'It's around nineteen-hundred,' she said, and found a pretty gift-box and wrapping paper. He paid by credit card and she gave him a ten per cent discount as they were both in trade in the town.

She hoped that they were going to leave it on a strictly business footing, but he put an arm around her at the back of the shop. 'Kirsty, won't you come out with me again? Or visit me and we can listen to more music? I thought that we had something going between us.'

She was acutely embarrassed. 'We have. We're good friends.'

'That's not what I mean.'

His arm tightened and he pressed her against him. She could feel that firming in his groin that heralded erection. His eyes devoured her and his mouth came closer. She went limp in his arms and accepted his kiss.

She found that her attitude altered. It was an experienced kiss that spoke wonders of his ability to pleasure a woman. Soft at first, then persuasive, wooing her into parting her lips and letting him slip his tongue between them. Her own responded, answering that intimate caress, while her breasts tingled and her delta moistened. It didn't have the emotional impact of her encounters with Dirk, but there was no denying the promise of enjoyment.

Recovering her senses, Kirsty put her two hands against his chest and pushed. 'Really, Robert. Someone might come in.'

He chuckled. 'Would I care? Look here, Kirsty, we've got to talk. There's something I want to ask you. Come to my place tonight. I'll cook for us. Say about half past seven?'

Something was stopping her from agreeing, but she fought against it. There was no reason for her to refuse. 'OK. I'll be there.'

He leaned forward and pecked her on the cheek, put his mother's present in his pocket and left the shop. From then on Kirsty was too busy to think about him and it was lunchtime before she stopped work. She left Meg in control and headed towards the harbour to meet Gina and find a cafe.

'How did it go? I meant to be there at opening time, but got delayed by Seth wanting one last fuck.' Gina was looking cool, wearing a minute skirt that showed her neat butt and tanned legs to perfection, complete with high-heeled mules and a brief top that emphasized her rounded breasts.

'He's in there, is he? I thought as much.' Kirsty was glad for her friend, but a little jealous, too. Men were so fickle. Only a day or so ago it had been her he intended to shag.

She wondered if Dirk would be the same. Robert seemed of a different ilk, almost stuffily reliable. He'd not be screwing someone else behind her back. She sat at a table on the pavement under an awning, rested her elbow on the surface and cupped her chin in her hand. The start of the shop had been encouraging and she had sold several items, while a few more had been set aside for customers to collect later. She should have been on top of the world, but there was discontent nibbling at the back of her mind.

Gina seemed relaxed and Kirsty envied her. A new man was all it took to complete her happiness or so it seemed. 'Darling, you make life hard for yourself,' she said, eyeing Kirsty shrewdly.

'I don't. Well, not deliberately.'

'If I were you, pet, I'd go for Robert. Forget the mean, moody and magnificent Dirk.'

'You're not me. I fall in love. You don't.'

'And I'm better off for it.' Gina pulled the ashtray towards her and lit up a cigarette. 'Life is for fun. Sex is for fun. Not the heavy drama you make of it.'

'That's not fair. I can't help how I am.'

'And I wouldn't have you any other way. I love you for it and hate seeing you get hurt. Marry Robert if he asks you and I'll be a bridesmaid.'

Kirsty found this annoying. 'Oh, do shut up! I'm not marrying anyone. He hasn't asked me.'

'And if he did?'

'The answer would be no.'

But she thought about it again when she closed the shop at six o'clock and drove to the cottage. The front door closed behind her and the place was as lonely as the *Marie Celeste*. Gina was not there, having arranged to meet Seth. And this is how it will be when she is gone, she mused gloomily. Night after night, here by myself. Summer will be bad enough, but the winter doesn't bear contemplating.

She put away her food purchases and made a cup of tea, switched on the television and watched the news. She didn't expect to see Gina that night and almost decided to have a bath and go to bed. The phone trilled and she flew to it, heart banging. Might it be Dirk? It was Robert, reminding her that he was cooking. It was on the tip of her tongue to make an excuse, say she was too tired - anything, but the sound of his voice cheered her and she replaced the receiver on its rest and hurried to get ready.

There was time for a shower and she stripped and entered the stall. The spray was stimulating, cascading over her shoulders and body, drops hanging from her nipples, then running down to mingle with her pubic air. It was just too much and she couldn't resist aiming the jet at her crack, opening her legs a little and allowing it to play on her clitoris. She closed her eyes and pretended that it was Dirk's tongue. Swept along by pure sensation, she could almost see him in the shower with her. He'd be kneeling at her feet, naked and wet as she was. He'd part her lower lips and make her clit stand proud, then toy with it and suck it.

She opened her eyes a fraction, fully expecting to see him there in reality. He wasn't but, just for a split second she caught a glimpse of him in the mirror tiles. Not only him. Lucian was smiling at her, too, and it was a smile of undisguised lechery. She started, blinked and they were gone. The jet tantalized her bud. She couldn't stop stimulating it. The feeling was growing in intensity, taking over completely. She rode the roller coaster to the heights, shattered into orgasm and plunged down again, shaking and gasping.

'She's a goer, all right.' Lucian wiped his cock and replaced it in his linen trousers. 'I see why you find her irresistible. Talk about wank material! That was a truly superb spurt I just had.'

Dirk was still holding his penis, his hand creamy with spunk. They had been watching Kirsty in the crystal ball, one of Lucian's favourite toys that he kept in Dirk's vault. He hadn't wanted to take part in this voyeurism, but had been unable to resist. Lucian was persuasive, sweet-talking even the most obstinate person into doing things his way. He appeared to have accepted that Dirk was determined to keep Kirsty out of it. But he couldn't stop teasing him, and the sight of her masturbating had been too much for the self-control of either of them. Feasting on her, they had whipped out their cocks and massaged them, fondled and rubbed them and brought about mind-blowing climaxes.

'Now she's off to see Robert,' Lucian remarked, pouring a shot of whiskey. 'How do you feel about that?'

Dirk slumped in a chair, a brooding expression on his ace. 'Not happy, though it's best for her. I can bring her nothing but misery and I won't put that on her.'

'Not even to save your immortal soul?' Lucian held up the glass to the light and squinted at the amber liquid. You may not get another chance for hundreds of years. Gabriel's a busy angel and can't always be at your beck and call.'

'I don't expect it to be. All I know is that Kirsty could be the one to fall so deeply in love with me that she'd be willing to make the ultimate sacrifice and I don't want to be the cause of her death.'

'How noble,' Lucian scoffed, but there was a savage glint in his eyes.

'Aren't you pleased that you're not going to lose your hold on my soul?'

'Of course, my dear. I should miss you.' Though Lucian sounded sincere, Dirk knew him well enough never to trust a word he said.

'Nothing will make me change my mind.'

'Shall we watch the love-birds together tonight? He has asked her around to his place for dinner and he's going to propose.'

'Good. I'm pleased for her and wish her well.' Pain lanced Dirk but he didn't show it.

'So the status quo will be restored and we can carry on as before,' Lucian said smugly.

Dirk was overcome by weariness. It was as if the three hundred plus years of wandering had suddenly hit him. He longed to lay his head on Kirsty's breasts and have her soothe him to sleep, waking to find her still there, a real person not some impermanent shadow.

He stood up and crossed to the window. She wasn't far away, getting ready for Robert. I won't interrupt them tonight, he vowed. I'll not use magic tricks and hope that Lucian won't either. Kirsty must be given freedom of choice. If she wants Robert, then so be it.

'It's so nice to have you here.' Robert opened the door for Kirsty and ushered her into his immaculately decorated house. Like most men living alone, it was neat to the point of coldness, lacking those little individual touches that a woman imparts to make it into a home.

She wished he hadn't used the 'nice' word, recalling what Gina and she had talked about. He took her wrap and she followed him into the dining room. He had spent time and effort setting the table. There were candles and a white damask cloth and folded napkins. Roses filled a vase, their fragrance wafting from the heavy scarlet blossoms. He was treating her as if she was visiting royalty and it warmed her heart.

'Would you like a drink before we eat? Red or white wine?'

'White, please.'

She speculated on just how many men would be so courteous once they had lured a woman to their lair. Many would simply dispense with formality and set about getting into her panties with all speed. Robert's caring attitude was endearing. No doubt part of his seduction ploy. Stop being so cynical! She chided herself. There are bound to be some decent men around.

They sipped the wine and she flipped through his collection of CDs. He joined her, pointing out this recording or that. He was very knowledgeable and she responded eagerly, glad to find someone who shared her taste in music. We could be happy together, she thought, then followed this with, but there's so much more to a relationship than being culture vultures.

'Dinner is ready.' He pulled out a chair for her and then disappeared towards the kitchen.

It was pleasant to be waited on and she couldn't fault his cooking. 'Where did you learn to produce such perfect dishes?' she asked at one point.

'My ex wasn't domesticated. She was a high-flyer. A career woman. I enjoy preparing meals and attended cookery classes run by Harry. He did a six week course in London and I took time out from selling houses. It didn't save my marriage, but has made me self-sufficient. I'm not seeking a housekeeper, Kirsty, but I would like wife.'

The intensity in his eyes made her feel uncomfortable and she ignored this last remark. 'Can I help you clear up?'

'No need. I'll stack it in the dishwasher. Make yourself comfortable and I'll bring in the coffee.'

The settee was deeply buttoned and old-fashioned, a genuine piece from the Edwardian era. Kirsty admired it. He placed the tray of coffee on a low table close by, and then put on a CD. She recognized the powerful, stormy music.

'That's Wagner.'

'The overture to *The Flying Dutchman* opera. Doesn't he capture marvellously the might of the sea, the winds and tempest and the tortured soul of the hero?'

She had heard it often before, but never had it had such an impact. Terrifying visions rose behind her eyes, and it was as if she was there on the battered sailing ship and a man stood beside her. She couldn't see his face. The overture concluded on a tranquil note. It portrayed dawn breaking and peace descending.

She had been so absorbed in the music that she was hardly aware of Robert. He had moved closer to her, his arm resting about her shoulders. He pressed the remote and the CD stopped. Silence fanned down and he said, 'Kirsty, will you marry me?'

Pain squeezed Dirk's heart like a huge, merciless fist.

He knew that he was a fool to watch her in the crystal, but couldn't help himself. Lucian had left him to it, sneering and going about his business in the universe. Unfortunately, there was no knowing when he might pop back.

Now Dirk saw Kirsty sitting with Robert, heard the wild music that he, too, knew well, and was devastated by Robert's words. Overwhelming rage possessed him and he only just prevented himself from cursing Robert and causing a heart attack, anything that would stop him in his tracks.

'No,' whispered a voice in his ear. 'This isn't down to you. His time has not yet come. Relax, Dirk, and let Saint Michael or Thoth if you prefer, the Keeper of the Records, examine his destiny, and yours and Kirsty's.'

From the corner of his eye, Dirk caught a flash of white and gold and recognised Gabriel. One doesn't argue with an angel. He bowed his head and uttered a silent plea, 'Help me.'

No one replied and he poured himself a large Scotch and walked out into the dusk, shrouding himself in it and warding off hope. It was a waste of time. There was no hope of redemption for someone like him.

Kirsty had been half expecting Robert's proposal, but when it came she was unsure what to say. The lame excuse sprang to her lips, 'Oh, Robert... I don't know. I'm honoured to be asked, but give me time to think about it. I haven't known you long.'

He smiled at her. 'Well, at least this isn't a downright refusal. Take all the time you want. I'm happy to know that I stand a chance.'

'Oh, you do! It's me being silly. I was let down badly by Martin. Now I want to be sure.' She hated to hurt him and felt that she was throwing him this sop as consolation.

She hadn't entirely dismissed the idea of marrying him. It would solve so many of her problems, the greatest of which was her attraction towards men who were bound to destroy her. She was tired of this, longing for security and when he leaned over and kissed her, she responded.

He lifted his lips from hers. 'Will you stay here tonight? I can offer you the guestroom.' His eyes burned into hers, filled with longing and the fear of rejection.

Why not? She thought. What have I got to go home for? An empty house. An empty bed.

Without giving herself a moment to think it through, she said, 'Yes, I'll stay, and don't worry about it. I'll sleep with you, if you like.'

It was as if she had offered him the sun, moon and stars. He couldn't do too much for her. They drank and listened to more music and he held her tightly in his arms as if afraid she was going to melt away. In the end, filled with alcoholic courage and savoir-faire, it was she who led the way upstairs.

His room was totally different to Dirk's and she was thankful. Plain and functional, it was tastefully decorated. There was a shower en suite, and he used it while she sat on the bed and remembered how she associated showers with Martin's betrayal. She had had too much to drink and lay back among the pillows, half asleep by the time Robert returned.

Going to bed with a new man is always a strange experience. Unlike Gina, Kirsty hadn't done it often. Being tipsy helped. Robert came into the room wearing a silk dressing-gown over pyjamas. She wasn't used to this. Martin had always gone to bed nude. She realised that she still wore her clothes and, made awkward by drink more than embarrassment, started to undress.

Robert took off his robe and the pyjama jacket but retained the pants. He was smiling broadly as if unable to believe his luck. The mattress sagged on one side as he sat down, rolled over and took Kirsty in his arms. He leaned back a little to admire her and she found it pleasant and friendly, if not madly exciting. This was not the case with him. His erection was fully fledged. Kirsty inveigled her hand into the fly and held it in her palm. It was large, hot and circumcised. He groaned and her fingers were sticky with his pre-come. Now she began to feel warm inside, her body responding.

He pressed her to him, kissed her eyes, her cheeks, her ears and her mouth, his hunger for her unrestrained. She felt small in comparison to his large frame, immensely comforted and secure. He had his own personal smell, nothing like Martin's or Dirk's. It didn't excite her like theirs had done, but it was pleasant. She waited for the ache in the womb, the tingle throughout her nervous system that heralded sexual arousal. Nothing. It was like being hugged by a friend.

It was obvious that he was expecting all the right signals, and when he started to caress her breasts and rub over the nipples, pleasure flooded through her, an automatic response as he found her erogenous zones. Dirk faded from memory, nothing mattered at that moment except Robert bringing her to orgasm.

He was skilful, knowing which buttons to press, his hands seeking and stroking her spine, ribcage, hungry breasts and then sliding down to cup her mound and insert a finger in her cleft. It was joyous and uncomplicated. She was intent on physical sensation, not caring if she was pleasuring him. He rubbed each side of her labial wings, made them slippery wet with her dew and then concentrated on her swollen clit. She moaned, gripped him hard, dug in her nails, and knew without doubt that he wouldn't fail her.

He was sucking her nipples as he kept up the rhythm on her nubbin, and the twin feeling rushed through her. 'I'm coming, Robert,' she whispered, gasping as she rose to the highest peak and convulsed into the most tense climax.

'That's it, my darling. All I want to do is give you pleasure.' He allowed her to come down from the heights and then positioned himself to enter her.

She welcomed him, needing a large prick to fill her and give her muscles something to clench around. Robert took his weight on his hands and knees and penetrated her with sure, swift strokes. His consideration was sweet and she gave herself up to him, wanting to lavish as much pleasure on him as he had just given her. There was no doubt as to her feelings for him, but she was sad to recognize that they weren't ones of passionate love. That terrible, wonderfully romantic emotion of falling 'in love' just wasn't there.

She lay still as his movements quickened, the expression on his face that of a martyred saint. Faster and faster he went and she braced herself until finally he gave a sharp bark and she felt the heat of his spunk filling her. He sighed and slumped across her, and she eased herself into a more comfortable position. She felt good.

That feeling continued even after he got up and insisted on making tea, bringing it back to bed where they talked as if they had known one another for years. He offered everything she could possibly need; companionship, affection, the promise of a solid marriage and possibly the children that they both wanted.

Later they cuddled up to one another in bed, her spine curved into his chest and her buttocks pressed against his belly, his cock between her thighs. It stirred and he fingered her pussy and gave her another orgasm before taking his own fill of her again.

'Marry me,' he insisted.

Full of spunk and heat and a delirious sense of well-being, 'All right. I will,' she said.

Dirk knew that Robert and Kirsty had mated. He had refrained from watching, but felt it in his bones, not to mention his soul. She was the kind of woman who wouldn't give her body lightly. Now that she had switched allegiance she was lost to him forever. He sat on the cliff edge under the light of the full moon. It hung there like a severed head, its features distinct, the mountains, valleys, volcanic craters. Nothing had changed ever since he had first become aware of it as a child.

Depression swamped him. All he could do was continue with his search. He couldn't even throw himself on to the rocks below and end it all. He was barred from this blessing.

'Why are you sitting there wallowing in self-pity?' He started as Lucian's instantly recognizable voice spoke just behind him. 'All right, so she's fucked someone else. Forget it. There's a party at a celebrity's house tonight. It should be a good one with lots of work for me... drugs, sex and rock-and-roll! Let's go.'

The location was London, a penthouse apartment overlooking the River Thames. They were there in an instant. Lucian was greeted rapturously by the host, an up-and-coming star of films and TV.

'I'm so glad you could make it,' he shouted, even more handsome than usual, a gorgeous woman on one arm and a dazzlingly beautiful transvestite on the other.

'I wouldn't miss it for worlds,' Lucian gushed. 'Do you know my friend, Dirk Stratten?'

'I do now.' He seized Dirk's hand in a firm grip, holding it a fraction too long as he said, 'I'm Perry... Perry Rand.'

Dirk freed himself as soon as it was politely possible. He had heard of Perry, a young man who had shot to fame in a celebrity show. The media adored him, at the moment, though able to turn on him like a pack if wolves should he suddenly drop from favour. These parties wearied Dirk. At one time he had gone along in the hope of meeting the woman who would save him, but as the years went by, he had come to believe that people were becoming increasingly selfish, greedy and materialistic. The milk of human kindness seemed to have dried up.

A rock band was playing. It consisted of good-looking, talented twenty-year-old lads whose first CD had topped the charts. 'They appeal to either sex and ride on both buses, if rumour is to be believed,' Lucian murmured in Dirk's ear.

'Is this supposed to impress me, maybe even stir my testosterone?' Dirk muttered, glancing around at the glamorous people, the budding stars, rising celebrities, producers, directors, all indulging in the alcohol, the cannabis and snorting the liberal bowls of cocaine. 'I see they're well into the Bolivian Marching Powder.'

'My goodness, we are in a sullen mood, aren't we?' Lucian teased, then grabbed him by the arm and propelled him across to where a queue of lovely girls waited to enter an anteroom. They were wearing transparent nightgowns, every curve showing, each pert nipple and the different shades of floss on their pubic mounds.

They genuflected when they saw him, crying, 'Master, master, we await you.'

'Not much longer, my pets. And I've brought you another playmate, too,' he replied encouragingly, and led Dirk through the door.

It was a small room, draped in crimson silk, with two chairs in the centre. The lighting was subdued. 'What are you up to now?' Dirk was suspicious.

Lucian chuckled and occupied one of the chairs. 'Sit down, dear boy. Make yourself comfortable. We are about to perform a service for those eager young ladies.' He turned to Barend, who had suddenly materialised. 'Call them in, two by two.'

A plump brunette and a willowy redhead entered timidly, though the dark beauty seemed familiar with the scene. She fell to her knees at Lucian's feet, crying, 'Will you do me, master? Only you!'

He thrust his hand into her hair and pulled her up, piercing her with his wild eyes. 'Greedy girl! Who gave you permission to speak? I've had you once and don't wish to repeat the experience. You will go to Mr Stratten, and perform well for him or it will be the worse for you.'

'Yes, master. I'm sorry, master.' At once she stood before Dirk, jiggling her full breasts.

'She's begging for a thrashing. Put her out of her misery,' Lucian advised, while the Titian haired girl spread herself across his knees, her bottom raised in supplication. 'That's what they queue for, the dirty little sluts. Convent school educated, the daughters of lords and politicians, they are no better than bitches on heat.'

'And you are doing them a favour and getting nothing out of it yourself? I don't think so.' Dirk was sceptical, though his sexual appetite was rising at the feel of the girl's thigh pressing against his groin.

He was smouldering with anger and this was transmuted into desire. Kirsty and Robert, engaged to me another. She had betrayed the true feelings that lay asleep within her, trampled on the love she felt. But didn't you tell her to do this? Dirk asked himself. Weren't you willing to sacrifice your own salvation to save her? It vas true, and he couldn't deny it. Why try? Why not indulge in every vice and pleasure? Kirsty meant nothing to him. Nothing!

His willing victim wriggled on his lap, her dark locks falling to the floor, her lithe body demanding his attention. He could feel her breasts rubbing against his leg, and caught a whiff of her scent - French perfume mingled with oceanic female love-juice.

It was a potent mix that went straight to his gonads. He heard the impact of Lucian's palm on the redhead's bare backside, accompanied by her shriek of pain and excitement. This inspired him to raise his own right land and bring it down with stinging force on the rounded rump of the whimpering girl stretched across his knees.

He struck her several times on each reddening cheek, making them ripple and swing while she squirmed against his crotch and his cock was hard as steel, weeping milky tears, needing to come, but restrained by memories of Kirsty.

Lucian's girl was mewling like a randy cat and, while he continued to slap her, one hand was under her crotch and her voice rose higher as he brought her to the ultimate pleasure. This affected Dirk's victim who cried, 'Bring me off, master! Please, please! Beat me some more and rub my clit!'

This was the last straw. Dirk tumbled her to the floor and stalked away, leaving her writhing, with her hand clasping her cunt as she worked herself to an orgasm.

'Get you!' Gina expressed her surprise and pleasure at her friend's news. 'Congratulations are in order. Engaged, eh? Well, well. Have you got a ring yet?'

'Robert is taking me to Penzance to buy one today. He wants me to choose. Money is no object, apparently.'

Gina looked up sharply. There was something missing in Kirsty's voice. It was too matter-of-fact and not rapturous enough. She doesn't love him, she concluded. Damn it! She's still hankering after Mr Mysterious of Rosewood Manor. She went on to ponder what it was about that kind of man that drew women to him like a magnet? Mr Rochester, Mr Darcy, Heathcliff, Rhett Butler - not quite respectable or the sort of husbands that their mothers would choose for them. They'd probably want them for themselves!

On the surface Kirsty seemed calm, having not long arrived at the shop. She had been back to the cottage and changed first. Although Gina had been fully occupied with Seth, she hadn't failed to note that her bed had not been slept in. Then she had dropped the bombshell. Robert had asked her to marry him and she had accepted.

Then why aren't I over the moon with happiness for her? Gina reflected, saying aloud, 'Is that Meg person, your assistant, going to mind the store?'

'She is indeed. Robert and I are going to have lunch and look around the port made famous by Gilbert and Sullivan. That's where they set their comic opera *The Pirates of Penzance*.'

'Great,' Gina said encouragingly, though no fan of G&S. Beside the tendency to fall in love, one thing that she and Kristy did not have in common was anything even vaguely approaching classical music.

'It will be,' Kirsty's voice was singularly lack-lustre and she was making quite unnecessary adjustments to the window display.

'There's something not quite right here. Tell your old Auntie Gina all about it,' she suggested, keeping the mood light.

To her astonishment, Kirsty rounded on her, very irritated. 'Of course there's nothing wrong! Get lost, Gina!'

Whoops! I touched a raw nerve there, Gina concluded to herself and left her to it.

'Shall we drive to the nearest town?' Lucian suggested cheerfully. He was bright-eyed and bushy-tailed and Dirk wondered how he managed to do it, even after a heavy night like the one just passed. It was another proof of his immortality.

'Why?' He asked listlessly. No matter how many gorgeous women had offered themselves willingly to him, nothing had eased the pain of Kirsty's engagement.

'Don't be such an old misery-guts. Let's visit the artists' colony in St Ives, or even Penzance. I fancy myself as a pirate king, don't you, old boy? I'd be as swashbuckling as dear old Errol Flynn. Now there was a guy who knew how to enjoy himself. Pity you haven't more of his spirit, Dirk.'

'You're seventy years out of date, Lucian.' Dirk's lip curled scornfully. 'Johnny Depp is the swashbuckler now.'

Lucian jumped down from the balustrade where he had been perched like some large bird of prey. 'Who fares? Where's your sense of adventure? Might pay you to follow your sweetheart and her fiancé. They're off to get the ring! I'm sure we can blight the occasion if we put our minds to it. What d'you say?'

Dirk knew what he *should* say, and that was to leave her alone, but the desperate yearning to possess and hold her prevented him. He shrugged and Lucian took this as assent. Within a short time they were bowling along the narrow Cornish lanes, driven by Barend.

If there was any part of the world that Dirk favoured, it was this stretch of English coast. He had been glad to find a house there and, if he could have done so, would have contemplated settling forever. When meeting Kirsty for the first time, he had permitted himself the indulgence of dreaming that this might be the case. Lucian had soon shown him that it was unlikely to happen.

Whilst watching the rugged landscape, where the trees grew crooked, leaning away from the prevailing wind, Dirk allowed himself the perverse pleasure of imagining walking into the jewellers where Robert was purchasing a diamond ring for Kirsty. This would put the cat among the pigeons, for she would be there, pretending to be overjoyed, while deep within her she would be wanting *him*, her true beloved.

Penzance was picture-postcard-pretty, filled with tourists enjoying the warm weather and strolling round the old fishing port, half believing the legend perpetrated by the operetta composers. That it had been the haunt of smugglers was true enough, and this gave it an added romantic atmosphere. The harbour side was lined with gift shops and cafes, stores selling T-shirts and surfboards, peppermint rock and bathing gear. Steep, narrow streets led down to this hub of activity, and where there had once been a thriving industry centred on produce from the sea, now the locals let out their houses or took in paying guests. They made all they could through the summer season, knowing that it would go quiet during the Autumn and winter.

Barend parked the car and was ordered to stay and guard it. While Lucian and Dirk strolled along the quay they attracted the attention of the women they passed, and several gay men as well. Strikingly handsome in shorts, T-shirts and terrain sandals, both were muscular and bronzed and had an exciting, predatory ambience about them that was irresistible.

Every woman gave them a second glance. Lucian was amusing himself by making their admirers' clothes transparent so that he could describe their attributes to Dirk. 'Look at that chick over there. Underneath her kaki shorts she has a perfect arse, rounded and with a deep crack that simply cries out for buggering. She isn't natural blonde. Her bush is brunette. And you should see the tits on that one! They're not implants, and what a luscious pair! I don't care for false ones, prefer the real thing.'

'I wish you'd belt up or go shag one of 'em! I don't want to hear it. OK?' Dirk clenched his fists into white-knuckled balls, longing to hit that smiling, sardonic face. Sometimes he could tolerate Lucian, but on days like today he found his presence maddening.

The trouble was, he never could deny him. If Lucian made a suggestion, then he found it impossible to refuse. Dig in his heels though he might, the fiend got his way. Like today's trip that was going to cause him pain. He could barely keep his rage under control, and this settled into a cold fury when he turned a corner and saw Robert and Kirsty hovering outside a jeweller's window.

Lucian's fingers dug into his arm. 'Come on. Into this delightfully old-fashioned tearoom. I'll bet they sell scones, with strawberry jam and clotted cream. Don't fret. The love-birds will come in, after they've made their purchase.'

The cafe was charmingly furnished with small round tables covered in red-and-white check cloths. There were net half-curtains at the windows facing the street, and Dirk saw Kirsty enter the jewellers with Robert. He cursed under his breath. A waitress in black, with a spotless apron and cap, came over to take their order. 'You want to see what's happening over there?' Lucian clicked his fingers and Dirk was standing behind the couple, while the assistant produced trays of rings from a showcase. He was a smooth-talking seller, knowing his trade.

Dirk was invisible, showing no reflection in the surrounding mirrors. Even so, Kirsty started and looked around, distracted from the sparkling diamonds displayed for her. 'Perhaps madam would like to try?' suggested the assistant, holding one out to her almost reverently. 'This is a quality stone and the setting should be about your size. If not, we can always alter it.'

It stabbed Dirk in the heart to watch her trying it on, turning her hand to make the diamond flash. He caught her disinterest and was glad, in spite of his resolutions. She didn't want Robert to buy her a ring and was forcing herself to accept him.

Robert admired it, but asked the salesman, 'Is there anything better? I'm not worried abut the price.'

Hearing this, the man became obsequious, very nearly fawning. 'Well, yes, sir. Excuse me a moment.'

He ordered a minion to keep an eye on the customers, and turned his attention to a wall panel that concealed a safe. From there he drew a small black velvet box and, having closed the safe securely, brought it over to the counter. With an air of pride that suggested he had manufactured the contents himself, he flipped open the lid. Dirk heard Kirsty gasp as she saw the magnificent ring inside.

'That's more like it.' Robert was impressed. 'Put this one on, darling.'

Will she sell herself for diamonds? Dirk thought, his anger mounting. She wouldn't take gems from me when offered them. But in his experience down the centuries, he had found that most women were venal. It was only their fear of committing themselves to his terms that had prevented them from sharing his fate.

Kirsty's hand shook as Robert slipped the ring on her finger. She stared at it as if mesmerized. 'It's perfect,' he said.

'It could have been made for you, madam,' agreed the assistant. Robert had not even asked how much. Dirk entered her mind, and witnessed avarice warring with love, decency clashing with the emotions that were ripping her apart. Weariness and the longing for security were wearing her down, while she strove to blanket what she felt for him, denying her true soul-mate.

She was weakening. Dirk felt that he had already lost her. Robert was a strong man and determined to get his way and it was this, more than the valuable gem that made her capitulate. 'It's lovely,' she murmured, taking it off and handing it back to the assistant.

'We'll take it.' Robert was decisive, already producing his credit-card.

Dirk followed them as, with the precious ring in its box safely in Robert's pocket, he heard him say, 'I'll fetch the car and we'll find a restaurant, have lunch and then go for a romantic drive where I can pull into somewhere secluded and slip the ring on your wedding finger, darling.'

He seemed unaware that Kirsty was agitated and needing space, saying, 'I'll pop into that dress shop there. You come and pick me up.'

He bent and kissed her as if he already owned her then walked jauntily down the street. Dirk slipped into his body that was still seated by Lucian who chatting up the waitress.

'I've invited this young lady to come to one of our parties at Rosewood Manor.' He winked at Dirk, aware of what had been taking place.

'I don't think I could get away.' She was embarrassed and flattered. 'My boyfriend wouldn't like it.'

'Bring him, too.'

Dirk wasn't listening, a red mist floating before eyes, his rage sweeping over him in a tidal wave. Robert had a ring that he intended to place on Kirsty's finger, marking her as his own! In spirit he rose above Penzance, following Robert as he headed for the car-park. Barend was still there, leaning against the limo, smoking a cigarette. The sun glistened on chrome and highly polished surfaces and Robert was there, getting into his car and starting up. Dirk's immortal eyes pierced metal and cloth and saw the ring, glittering in the darkness of its box.

He caught a glimmer of white and gold, but ignored Gabriel, shutting his mind to the voice that said, 'Don't do it, Dirk.'

The car wheeled out of the parking lot, heading for the road that would bear Robert to the dress shop. There was a bang and a clash of metal as another vehicle travelling at speed down the hill, hit him with shattering force.

Chapter Seven

This is all my fault, Kirsty mourned as she arrived at the scene of the accident a few moments after hearing the crash.

She pushed her way to the front of the crowd. The police were there, and ambulance-men gathered around Robert's crumpled car. There didn't appear to be much damage to the other one and its driver was talking with the cops. Robert's vehicle was a write-off and he lay on a stretcher, apparently unconscious.

'His name is Robert Caldecote and I'm his fiancée.' She addressed one of the officers. 'Is he badly injured? What happened?'

'As far as we can tell, he has a broken leg and head injuries, nothing too serious. The driver of the other car says he lost control of the brakes and couldn't stop.'

Kirsty was permitted to drive in the ambulance with Robert, who had not yet regained consciousness. Time had no meaning, and she stayed with him while he was examined, his head and leg x-rayed, the former operated on, and then he was put to bed in a side-ward. He opened his eyes, saw her and woke fully.

'How did I get here?' He was dazed and in pain.

'It's OK, Robert. You had a car accident and have broken your left leg. Give me your house key and I'll fetch your pyjamas and shaving kit.' She felt brisk and efficient and no way alarmed. It was what she would have offered to do for any friend who had met with misfortune.

'Where are my clothes?' He had been changed into a hospital gown.

'In the locker by your bed.'

'Take the ring. I can remember buying it. Take and wear it.'

There was nothing she could do but agree, then kissed him and left. He looked somehow shrunken, lying in the narrow bed. She was recovering from the shock and took a taxi back to her cottage. Glancing across at Rosewood Manor, as she always did when entering her bedroom, she was suddenly struck by the thought, Dirk had something to do with this. How dare he?

He wanted his own way and, even while denying her love, couldn't bear anyone else to have her. She fully believed him capable of almost anything, like paying someone to interfere with Robert's engine. But it was the other car whose brakes failed, she remembered and felt a chill run down her spine. She put the ring in a drawer and locked it, then realised that he would be upset if she wasn't wearing it when she next visited, she got it out and slid it on her finger. It felt hot as if the gold band was burning. Kirsty ignored this, and went to Robert's home and gathered items he would need.

'How awful! D'you want me to come back and help?' Gina grabbed Craig's cock, preventing him from trying to insert it into her. It was late at night, but she was too busy with her telephone call to bother with him. 'How's Robert doing?'

'He's OK, thank God. All being well, he'll be out at the end of the week, but on crutches. His head seems OK, just minor lacerations.'

'Will you be at the hospital much? Can Meg manage the shop?'

'I'll visit him during the evenings, but he'll need me more when he comes home, I guess.'

'Give me a day to sort things out here and then I'll be with you. If I wasn't a modern-thinking woman I might imagine that Dirk put a hex on him. I'll bet he was good and mad when he heard about your engagement.'

There was a split-second pause, and then she heard Kirsty say, 'That's a load of bull, and you know it.'

'If you say so, but it wouldn't do any harm to have a little chat with him.'

'I've already decided that I will. Goodnight, Gina. See you.'

'Goodnight, pet. Sleep well.'

'You're not going away again, are you?' Craig sounded petulant.

That's the only drawback of getting 'em young. They get dependent, Gina mused, ruffling his hair, making soothing noises and saying, 'I shan't be gone long. Must keep an eye on Kirsty. You remember her, don't you? Her guy's just been involved in a car accident.'

This seemed to satisfy him and he snuggled into her, rousing her as she had trained him to do, using those little erotic tricks that delighted her. She wondered how she could possibly leave all this pleasure behind, then remembered Seth and his more experienced form of fucking. Why not enjoy the best of all possible worlds?

I'm not cut out for this, Kirsty thought crossly, as she prepared for yet another trip to the hospital.

She was sorry for Robert and felt responsible, though not knowing why. Finding a place to park the car, tramping endless corridors to the right ward and then trying to make conversation was an unnatural way of carrying on. Normally, one did not sit for an hour by someone's bed mouthing small talk. The fact that he was in a private ward made it worse, for there was no one else with whom to pass the time of day. Just her and Robert, with him gazing adoringly at her and full of wedding plans. There would be an engagement party as soon as he was fit again. He was eager to show her off to his friends.

When she arrived that day the doctor was there, nice looking and she had already spotted him. As she came in, he turned to her with a warm smile. 'He's doing very well. You should have him home by the weekend.'

Kirsty was smitten by guilt as she met Robert's delighted grin. 'That's great,' she responded, sitting on the side of the bed, while he took her hand in his and squeezed her fingers.

When they were alone, he pulled her towards him and kissed her full on the lips. His tongue caressed hers and she could feel his eagerness. He threw back the quilt. 'Get in with me.'

'Stop it, Robert. Someone might come in.'

He was insistent, loving every moment of this wealth of attention. In an instant, he had grabbed her hand and pushed it down the front opening of his pyjama pants. 'Don't deny a sick man.' His grin was infectious.

She relented, cruising past his navel and pubic hair and grasping the erect phallus. 'I've heard it said that men get a hard-on until the very end,' she teased, stroking it, her fingers sticky with pre-come.

She relaxed. It was really very pleasant there, so clean and sterile with the sun shining in through the open windows and flowers arranged in vases. How different to her encounters with Dirk in his lair. Beautiful and old though it was, it had frightened yet aroused her. The hospital room was wholesome, and so was Robert. No mystery there. What you saw was what you got.

'Sit astride me. It's my leg that's broken, not my cock. Have you a johnny in your bag, by any chance?'

'As a matter of fact I have. Since meeting you, I thought it wise, as you're often impulsive,' she countered, hoping this explanation would satisfy him. She pulled wide his pants and removed her own, working the condom on to his cock, then hoisting up her skirt and settling herself on his belly. She would feel his dick behind her, as rigid as a broom-handle. He slid his hands under her crop-top and bra and cupped her breasts, rubbing the nipples. Pleasure flooded her. She played with her clit, and juice flowed from her. Robert's penis nudged her backside and she rose a little so that he could penetrate her vagina. She couldn't stop from riding him, while he massaged her clit. She was careful not to put pressure on his plaster encased leg.

'It's the first time I've fucked a hospital patient,' she gasped, the waves of feeling mounting from her belly, through her spine and up to her cortex.

Robert grunted, letting her do all the work. 'Go on... go on...' he urged.

So she was to do everything? Arouse her clit and his cock, completely in control? It was an odd, exciting situation. This is how a man must feel sometimes, master of all he surveyed. She took on the role gladly, bringing herself off first, and then bumping up and down on his phallus until he cried out and came.

'You didn't make a very good job of it, old boy.' Lucian's voice dripped with sarcasm. 'She's bloody well screwing him! Take a peek.'

Dirk wanted to refuse, but couldn't resist the scrying-glass. Lucian was right. Kirsty was astride Robert on the hospital bed, humping him for all she was worth. He felt the fury of her orgasm and saw him convulse in pleasure. Then she slid down, her head on Robert's chest, her breathing slowing.

That was where Dirk caught her; in that state of drowsiness preceding sleep. Her astral body rose to stand by the bed with him, looking down at her physical shell. Dirk held out his hands and took hers. She stared at him questioningly.

'How is it that you are here?' Her words reverberated in his brain.

'I am wherever I want to be. I simply think it and am there.'

'Who are you? What are you? Was it you who hurt Robert?'

'Come to Rosewood Manor tonight and I will explain everything.'

Kirsty slept and when she awoke, a nurse was walking in, bringing Robert's medication. She gave them a knowing glance, but made no comment on their dishevelled clothing. When he had been given an injection, a nursing auxiliary brought in tea and they drank it together and chatted until it was time for her to leave. It was only as she was driving home that she suddenly remembered her dream. Or was it a dream? Had Dirk really been there, inviting her to the manor?

Gina was waiting for her at Tregaskis Cottage, car parked outside, suitcase and laptop in the hall. 'Shit! You look worn out!' she exclaimed, hugging her.

She was like a breath of fresh air, and Kirsty realised just how tired she was, and admitted, 'It's no fun trying to run a business and visit the hospital to boost his morale. He's coming home at the weekend and I shall have to look after him, I guess.'

'Leave it to the professionals.' Gina switched on the kettle and got out the coffee and mugs. 'You know I'll do anything I can to help, like running the shop, but can't you get the district nurse to call in and do what's necessary?'

'Of course, and that's all in hand, but he's not bedridden or anything like that. He'll be on crutches and can get around slowly, but he'll need company, and that will be me.'

Gina, ever practical, suggested, 'Bring him here.'

This was a reasonable solution, but Kirsty was reluctant to get Robert installed in her domain. There was something so final about it. His slippers would be warming at her hearth before she knew it! 'I don't know,' she demurred. 'This is my place. I don't want him getting territorial.'

She came under the scrutiny of Gina's eyes. 'You're far from committed to him, aren't you? Still got the hots for Mr Mystery Man? Oh, God, Kirsty, what am I going to do with you?'

Kirsty shrugged. 'I'm not sure what I feel or for whom.'

'It's time you talked to him. Grab the bull by the horns, or by the bollocks.'

'OK, I'll go and see him. If he doesn't want me there, then I can always leave.' She didn't mention that dream state when he had invited her.

She floated through what remained of the day, unable to concentrate on anything. Gina went to find Seth, her encouragement a boost to Kirsty's courage. The evening shadows were lengthening, the sun a crimson disc on the horizon as she drove along the coast road, turning off for the manor. She was extremely nervous, but had the strange feeling that this was ordained. She had been fated to move to Cornwall and meet Dirk. There wasn't a thing she could have done about it, any more than stopping herself from falling in love.

He was waiting for her at the top of the steps and she glanced up as she went towards him. The setting could have been designed especially for him, Tudor arches, mullioned windows, gargoyles mounting guard on the guttering. She met his eyes as she reached him. He took her cold hands in his warm fingers. They didn't speak. There was no need for words. Once inside, the atmosphere of the house enfolded her, redolent of old happenings years ago yet imbued with the personality of its present owner. It seemed deserted, but then Lucian appeared out of nowhere.

'Kirsty.' He clicked his heels, gave an old-fashioned bow, then bore her hand to his lips.

It was more than a formal acknowledgement. As soon as he touched her skin, every nerve in her body quivered, concentrating in her loins. She withdrew her hand, awed by her reaction and resentful that he was present.

'Come into the games room.' Dirk led the way. 'It is time we talked.'

'And I can offer my advice.' Lucian followed them. Kirsty wished he'd go away.

It was a masculine den with hunting trophies adorning those walls that were not lined with maps and bookcases. A fire flickered in the grate, and lamps with silk shades standing on a wide desk and several plinths, sent out a rosy glow. Even so, a cold aura surrounded Lucian, who stretched out in a wing-chair, after pouring a measure in a brandy glass.

Dirk escorted her to a settee, but did not sit beside her. He was restless, pacing the carpet like a caged tiger. 'There are facts you should know,' he began.

'About you?'

'Exactly.'

'Before you start, there's a question I must put to you.'

'Fire away.'

Dear God, if only he wasn't so handsome! she thought despairingly, while saying, 'Were you instrumental in Robert's accident?'

Lucian laughed loudly, almost choking on his drink, but Dirk couldn't meet her eyes, muttering, 'Maybe.'

'Why?' She already guessed the answer, but had to ask.

'To stop you getting engaged to him.'

'Why?' she asked again.

'Because Dirk wants you to fall in love and give up your life for him.' Lucian had the smug look of a cat that has been at the cream.

Hope leaped like a bright flame within her. Dirk wanted her to devote herself to him and that could only mean he would ask her to be his wife. She rose from the couch. 'Is this true, Dirk? Then why did you tell me not to love you? Do you really think I would have accepted Robert, if I'd have known this was the case?'

'It's true. You'd have been safe with him, whereas you won't be with me, but I just couldn't help myself when I saw you in the jewellers with him.'

'So you were there? I thought I was dreaming.'

He nodded slowly, and she realised that every time she saw him on an unearthly plane, this was a reality and not a figment of her imagination. It was hard to accept, yet she wanted so much to do so. She had become sceptical of other-world experiences, astral travel, communing with spirits and reincarnation, even religion had seemed absurd, yet she was having to rethink her relationship with this man.

'Oh, get on with it, Dirk. This is boring. Say what you have to say and be done with it!' Lucian stood up impatiently, poised like a ballet dancer about to launch into a leap.

'Go away, then. I didn't ask you to be here!'

'Right! If you think you can manage without screwing it up, then I'm off.'

He was gone, not through the door or out of the window. He'd vanished into thin air.

'Where is he?' Kirsty stared around her, mystified.

'Don't bother about him. He comes and goes as he pleases.'

'Who is he?' She seemed to be full of questions that evening.

'He has many names. The Devil, Satan, Mephistopheles, Beelzebub, or Lucifer, Son of the Morning, God's favourite angel until he was kicked out for defying Him.'

'Oh, yes,' she said scornfully. 'Pull the other leg; it's got bells on it!'

'You think I'm joking? I'm telling the truth.'

'You expect me to believe you?' She spoke more forcefully than she felt. Doubts were sneaking into her mind. It couldn't be true, could it? Either he was mad or she was, or they both were!

'Why should I lie? And I'm telling the truth when I say that I have been roaming the planet for hundreds of years, condemned to wander because I sold my soul to him in exchange for satisfying my ungovernable pride.'

Kirsty sank back on to the couch, hoping he was teasing but fearful that he wasn't. 'And he has been your companion?'

'When it amuses him to be. He's a very busy fallen angel, but likes to keep in touch with me, play a game of dice, catch up on the gossip, seeing if I've found a woman willing to die for me, for this is my only hope of salvation and if it happens he will have to relinquish my soul.'

It was almost impossible to believe, but, 'You're the Flying Dutchman,' she whispered.

'Yes.' His voice was low.

'But you can't be. That's nothing but a legend, surely?' I *am* going crazy, she thought.

'Legends are often based on truth. Yes, I'm that proud captain who defied the Almighty and made a pact with Lucifer for the right to sail successfully around Cape Horn and become the most famous seamen of them all. Many sailors have sighted my battered vessel in the midst of storms, and spread the story far and wide.'

Kirsty knew the tale and now understood her place in it. 'You were promised to be released if a woman loved you so much that she was willing to die for you.'

'The Angel Gabriel made this concession, but Lucifer's confident that I shall never find such a one. There have been women in the past, but they have always shied away from paying such a price. When I met you, I knew that you would do this for me if I asked, but was unwilling to sacrifice you. I'd rather go on roaming through eternity than see you die.'

'But in death we would be together, surely?' Gone were the doubts and scepticism that had vexed her before.

She was standing close, looking up into his stormy, green-grey eyes, and trembling with the desire to be held by him, her soul-mate for all time. Any physical pleasure she had shared with Robert was as nothing. Dirk and she were one, maybe fulfilling some age-old contract or debt that needed to be paid. Whatever it was, she was prepared to go the whole mile and more.

With arms entwined, they mounted the staircase and went to his bedroom. Whatever happened in the future, they were determined to enjoy what time they had left. It was wonderful, an encounter filled with tenderness ad passion. Dirk laid her on his bed and carefully took off her clothes, as if he was unwrapping a precious gift. When she was naked, he didn't touch her right away, worshipping her with his eyes. And she watched him, filling herself with the sight of his perfect face with those chiselled features framed by his long black hair.

He sighed deeply, and then undressed and she gasped at the perfection of his muscular body. He resembled a piece of sculpture crafted by a master. Tanned, swarthy, his shoulders were wide, tapering to a narrow waist and tight buttocks and thighs. He had long legs and the physique of an athlete. Most women would have given their eye-teeth but not, apparently, their lives, to couple with him. Kirsty, deeply in love, was willing to do anything.

She melted into his embrace, his kisses honey-sweet yet masterful. He fondled her breasts and body, limbs and genitals, playing on her like a musical instrument bringing forth the sweetest sounds as she moaned her pleasure and used her own fingers to arouse him. Each touch expressed her love, wanting to give him the greatest sensations. He bent his dark head and kissed her mound, parting the labial wings and flicking her clitoris with his tongue-tip, his fingers still palpating her nipples. The triple sensations flared through her. She caressed his face and buried her fingers in his curls, unable to get enough of him. Everything about him was arousing, his looks, the personal odour of his body and hair, his skill at bringing her fulfilment.

At the height of her climax, he whispered, 'That's it, darling. Do it for me. Come for me... that's right... come.'

She rose to the peak, shuddering with the force of it, riding the rollercoaster to bliss. At the very moment when she was gliding down, he thrust into her, giving her inner muscles just what they needed to clench around. He moved slowly and deeply, his penis filling her to capacity, butting against her cervix, rubbing her G-spot, adding to her pleasure.

'Oh, Dirk,' she sobbed, unable to hold her emotions in check. 'I love you.'

'And I you, my darling. Forever and always.'

Lucifer, a wraith behind the bed-curtains, watched them, his face set in brooding, melancholy lines. He heard the soft brush of wings and Aphrodite appeared beside him, wearing the guise of an owl.

'Love is denied you.' She shook off her feathers and assumed her female form. 'Human love, warm and caring. No fireside or children, no wife or family.'

'I was once loved by the Creator.' He voiced a grievance aeons old.

'Your pride was your downfall, as was my mother's. Lilith refused to obey her husband, Adam. She was his first wife, but too lively and wild, and wanted to be on top when they mated, while he insisted she lay beneath him. God cast her out of Eden and gave him Eve instead. Poor old Eve, she took the blame for everything, but mother went off and gave birth to demons, including my sisters and I, the Lilim.'

'I know all this. She's a friend of mine. It's my very arrogance that makes me understand Dirk. I shall miss him if Kirsty succeeds. Oh, I have millions of souls in captivity and a host of demonic hordes to do my bidding, but no one to call friend.'

'Oh, come on! Never let it be said that Satan is prone to self-pity.' Aphrodite clasped him around the neck and wriggled her pliant body against him. There was a piquant whiff of sulphur about her, and Lucifer began to feel that things weren't so bad after all.

She resembled the feisty Lilith, and along with her sisters, had made an art of seducing men, their favourites being celibate priests to whom they gave wet dreams. Lucifer had a soft spot for her, but he was the Devil without a heart, and disliked the feeling that struggled to exist in his breast when he saw Kirsty giving her all to Dirk, not only her body, but every part of herself.

With his ability to become anything, he slipped into the bodies of the lovers as they reached their zenith. He shared their orgasms and struggled to share their emotions, but was baffled by their love. This he couldn't share, Lord of the Abyss though he was. It was a white, shining light that near blinded him and he took his leave abruptly.

Gina had a kind of sixth sense where Kirsty was concerned. 'She's shagging Dirk Stratten,' she remarked to Seth.

They had just finished eating in the main cabin of his boat, anchored in the harbour. He had asked her there for dinner, and had bought fish and chips from the shop on the quayside. Gina decided that there was nothing more glorious. The TV chefs could take a running jump! All their exotic concoctions were as naught compared to fresh cod fried in batter and sliced potatoes cooked to perfection in a Cornish chip shop.

He shrugged his muscular shoulders, filling their mugs with beer. 'So what?'

Kirsty lit a cigarette while he used a paper and tobacco to make one for himself. 'She's engaged to Robert.'

'When did that stop a good woman?' He applied a match to his roll-up.

'You rotten old cynic.' She ruffled his gypsy curls.

'I'm realistic, that's all.' He kissed her full on the lips.

Gina knew that she was in for a night of sex. They hadn't had the opportunity to do it there yet, but she appreciated the romantic setting of this rugged boat that had been in Seth's family for generations. He had proved to be a big softie after all, despite his tough exterior, unable to disguise his joy at seeing her again. Craig faded into the background. He was a bit too young anyway, and would probably find a girl of his own age soon.

She surfaced from Seth's kiss long enough to say, 'I'm seriously thinking of moving down here, sharing Kirsty's shop and cottage, but keeping on the place in Bath.'

'I'm glad. You mentioned it before but I didn't think you were serious.' He left the table and wandered across to the bunk that could be used for seating or, by pulling out an extension, as a comfortable double bed.

Gina wanted to try it. 'Make it bigger,' she urged. 'Then we can both lie on it.'

'Are you planning to sleep here?'

'I might be.'

He grinned at her and made the adjustments and the padded cushion at the back slid down to form an additional mattress. An under-sheet, duvet and pillows completed the transformation. He took over his beer and put it on the locker, then stretched out his long limbs and patted the space beside him.

'"Come to me arms, me bundle of charms,"' he said gruffly, in a piratical tone of voice.

Gina went over and he reached up to grip her around her waist and pull her roughly against him. She thrilled at his strength and the brush of his bearded jaw and the hardness of his muscles that made her feel puny and weak and utterly feminine. An unusual, pleasing sensation for she was normally in charge.

It was growing dark outside, the harbour lights gleaming on the water, the craft rising and falling lightly. Seth left her momentarily, taking a match to the oil-lamp that swung gently on its gimbal. When he returned, he was naked, clothes in a heap on the floor. He flung back the duvet. 'Get your kit off, and come here this instant, woman!'

Gina entered into the spirit of the game, letting him play the master. She stripped out of her jeans, T-shirt, bra and panties and lay back voluptuously. He was on her in a second, kneeling across her belly, her thighs between his, his hands each side of her face as he held her firmly and captured her mouth with his. His tongue was fleshy and her own responded. Moans issued from her throat and she wriggled her hips against him, aware of his balls in their hairy sac and his rock-hard cock.

He left her lips and trailed his tongue down her throat to her breasts, tantalising her nipples, then dropping past her navel to her bush, parting the crack with his fingers and subjecting her clitoris to a firm sucking. He was insistent and she had her first glorious climax. He entered her as she was coming down from it, and reached his own crisis. She clung to him, her arms around his back, fingertips exploring the tanned, slightly furred flesh. He was a rogue, no doubt, but this added to his attraction. Could she tame him? Did she want to? Time would tell, but just for the moment, she was content and prepared to join him in another bout. It occurred to her to wonder if Kirsty was faring so well.

'What happens now?' Kirsty lay in the crook of Dirk's elbow. They were resting after making love several times.

'Lucifer will be in touch. Undoubtedly he knows everything that has been said and done.' Dirk sounded weary, but content.

Their relationship seemed so normal that Kirsty had to keep reminding herself of the hazards. It would be so easy to pretend they were an ordinary couple who had just declared their love. Instead they were as much star-crossed lovers as Romeo and Juliet. For the first time in ages, she felt the need to pray. If there was a God, and these strange circumstances were forcing her to become a believer, then surely heavenly aid would come? Dirk had not done something terribly wicked, after all. He had been a fine seaman and an explorer, but she could not deceive herself. He had sold his soul to Satan to realise his ambition.

It was that still time of night that she knew as The Hour of The Wolf, when problems and fears were magnified, stalking through the darkness to haunt one. Dirk was asleep, his face relaxed, lines smoothed away, making him look somehow boyish. Kirsty leaned over and kissed him, then slipped into her clothes and left the room. Dawn wasn't far away, and a hush lay over all. The house was dimly lit, but Kirsty followed her instinct and found her way to the tiny chapel, once used by the family. She let herself in. The stained glass windows threw dim patterns on the tiles as she made her way to the altar. Thick white candles in brass sconces awaited her and she lit them. Peace descended on her, and she knelt and bowed her head, praying for forgiveness for Dirk and blessings on their love.

'You are the one we have been waiting for.' A voice spoke in her ear and Kirsty opened her eyes with a start. The person standing beside her reached out a hand and raised her to her feet.

'Who are you? How did you know I was here?' Kirsty was calm and no longer afraid, even though the visitor was surrounded by light so dazzling that it was hard to distinguish form or features.

'I am the Archangel Gabriel, the most feminine of the higher echelons. We thought you might need our help.'

'It was you who tried to intervene between Lucifer and Dirk at the start.'

'That's true, but there was little I could do. Dirk had made his choice and the transaction between him and Satan was already signed and sealed. Are you ready to die for him?'

'Yes, but I wish it wasn't so. I'd love to spend the rest of my life with him, and for us to die naturally.'

The angel shook her head, golden sparks flying. 'Satan has the last word on this. To make it even remotely possible you must go and visit him on one of the levels of Hell. Should he decide to be lenient, then he will have to fix it with the Angel Michael. He is the one who weighs the heart and helps to look at the path souls are to take in their next incarnation.'

She was so convincing that Kirsty could not argue. 'Tell me how to do this.'

The angel's face came into focus, beautiful and calm. 'You are brave, Kirsty, and love is like a flame within you. This is the greatest power of all. Never forget this. Now, to get down to practicalities. You'll need a guide to enter the realms of Hell. There is one waiting. She won't be a stranger to you. You've already met her, though her appearance may be odd at first. She can't come into the church. Wait for her beyond the gate, away from hallowed ground.'

Kirsty was alone. The nave rang with a queer emptiness, devoid of that powerful presence. This is rubbish! She thought crossly. Someone is messing about. If I find out it's Gina, I'll make her smart!

But she couldn't imagine Gina frightening her or playing such a dirty trick. If it wasn't a real person, then who was doing it? There was only one way to find out. Kirsty stepped from the church into the dewy stillness, and waited.

Chapter Eight

Kirsty shivered as she stood in the churchyard. Gabriel had gone and, what am I doing here? I must have taken leave of my senses, she thought. Angels? Satan? Lilith? Anyone would think I'd been on the wacky-baccy!

About to leave, she was stopped by the sound of hooting and the brush of wings as a large tawny owl swooped from one of the yew trees and landed beside her. It immediately turned into Aphrodite, that sensual blonde who had reigned supreme at the orgy in Rosewood Manor. She was wearing tight jeans that outlined her pert arse and the divide of her pussy, high heeled ankle boots and a sweater that displayed her perfect breasts, no silicon implants but the real thing.

'Hi, there.' She drew Kirsty into an embrace that was sexy and friendly all at the same time. 'I've been ordered to take you to His Satanic Majesty. We never did get it together, you and me, but there's still time. We're out of here.'

Kirsty sank into her, swallowed up in Aphrodite's plumage as she became a night-bird again, rising on smooth wings, reaching an incredible height, then levelling out and gradually starting to drop.

'Where are we?' Kirsty communicated with her mentally.

'Between universes. Heading for Lucifer's domain.'

'D'you mean Hell?'

'Not as you have been led to believe it. Like Heaven, there are many layers, many meanings. It is very complicated, but I'll tell you this for free... most religions include it... a place where sinners are punished. We're visiting our boy in one of his luxurious palaces, where he runs his business.'

'Is he expecting me?'

'Of course.'

Kirsty found herself staring down at a glittering spectacle, a city white as snow and cold as ice. There were towers rearing skywards, and domed buildings, wide avenues, and inhabitants such as she had never seen before. Aphrodite landed on a window ledge and pecked the glass with her beak. It melted and she flew inside. Kirsty was standing on a marble floor that stretched away into infinity. It resembled an office, with computers buzzing and operators clicking away at keyboards. None of them looked completely human or even animal. They kept changing shape. The place shone with a brilliant white light. Aphrodite and Kirsty glided across to where Lucifer sat at a monumental desk, several large screens before him. Each held a different scene, horrific war zones, politicians arguing, ravaged countries, children starving, pomp and ceremony as monarchs were crowned, natural disasters, earthquakes, tsunamis and hurricanes.

'This is how I keep watch on my domain,' he said, as if continuing a conversation Kirsty couldn't recall starting. He turned to Aphrodite and cupped her luscious breasts, no bird now, but a gorgeous female. In an instant they were coupling over the desk. He pushed her face down across it and wrenched off her jeans and thong, then he freed his cock and thrust it smoothly into her vagina. Clearly Aphrodite had been ready to receive him, but he withdrew it after only a few thrusts and shifted his aim. Kirsty watched the woman tense as she waited for what she knew was coming, watched the creature she had known as Lucian dig his fingers deep into the perfect cushions of her buttocks and then he rammed the thick column of his cock smoothly into her narrow channel and made her arch and cry out beneath him.

His lips curled into a cruel smile as he heard the sound, it obviously pleased him to make her suffer.

The computer operators ignored them, but Kirsty was impressed by the size of his dick, wondering how any woman could take such a huge tool into her. Despite Aphrodite's continuing groans, she had an urge to try. It sickened yet fascinated her. Part of her still thought she was dreaming, lying beside Dirk at Rosewood Manor.

Lucifer, as she now thought of him, withdrew his cock from Aphrodite's backside. His eyes were feline as he smiled at Kirsty. 'Why am I here?' she ventured. Aphrodite was no help, recovering almost instantly from her penetration, she was perched naked on the edge of the desk, buffing her nails.

'You know why. You want to persuade me to go easy on you and Dirk. It's not entirely down to me. I shall have to consult the Archangel Michael. He's in charge if things, but owes me a favour or two. And what do I get out of it, if I do this?'

'I don't know. You have everything, haven't you? I'm only human with nothing to offer.'

Lucifer's brightness faded, replaced by the dark, shabby figure of a man, shoulders bowed, hair greying, his face marked with sorrow. 'You know so little about me, Kirsty. Don't you think I miss the angels who were once my companions? I was used by the Creator to teach humans that if one only knows good, how can one recognize evil? I am the shadow side of Him, the ying of His yang, chaos contrasting with order. He has all he kudos and I get the shit flung at me.'

'Well, you don't seem to have done badly out of it,' Kirsty retorted sharply. 'I despise a devil who moans about his lot.'

He changed immediately, becoming a huge, hideous monster with a horrible leering face and flaming red eyes. Horns sprouted from his head and leathery wings sprang from his shoulders. He was paunchy, with goat's legs and enormous genitals, the balls swinging between his thighs, his phallus upward thrusting. Followers knelt before him, in human and inhuman form, worshipping, prostrating themselves, wanting to kiss his prick. Kirsty recognised some of them from the orgy. Aphrodite watched with glittering, snakelike eyes, observing Kirsty's reaction to this demonstration of power.

'Mind what you say, woman!' he roared, and one of his massive hands seized Kirsty's arm, his talons drawing blood. 'Your mockery will be punished. But first, see the various levels of my Kingdom.'

She was propelled towards the screen and saw souls streaming down into the Abyss where they were seized by demons and thrown into fiery pits or boiling oil, receiving the torture they believed they deserved. Their cries were agonised, their flesh sizzling, but unable to escape, condemned to suffer throughout eternity. The picture constantly changed. Icy regions blasted the unhappy spirits. They were buffeted by gales and hunted by demonic horsemen, and there was never any end or rest or redemption.

'But this isn't true,' Kirsty protested. 'Stories to frighten children.'

Lucifer clicked his fingers and the screen went blank. He was once more the suave, sophisticated gentleman. 'It can be whatever a person wants or expects. This is but a trifling display of my vast empire.' He slapped Aphrodite on the arse, saying, 'I think it's time we had a party, don't you? To celebrate the arrival of our guest.'

This is so much like the story of Alice, a twisted kind of Wonderland. Kirsty was puzzled by the thought, but realized that it was true enough. Things kept changing, in a continual state of flux. Lucifer's office melted, became different. *He* became different, an experienced shape-shifter. Just as she got used to him in one guise, so he assumed another. She knew he was teasing her and demonstrating his prowess, and she was gradually accepting it, though more comfortable when he became the elegant Lucian once more.

She had been transported to a ballroom, all glitz and glamour, plush upholstery, gilded furniture, with sparkling glitter-balls suspended from the ornate plaster ceiling. The floor was highly polished, reflecting the dancers. The orchestra was playing a waltz by a Strauss. Gentlemen in evening suits glided through the steps, leading their exquisitely gowned partners. It was like a movie set from the early nineteen-thirties, circumspect and romantic, depicting a story from an earlier era. Kirsty felt at home there, relieved that nothing untoward was happening. As far as she could tell, every item had been reproduced to perfection, although given Lucifer's influence, they were probably originals.

She didn't know how, but she was wearing a tight-waisted crinoline with a hoop skirt that swayed as she moved. The bodice was low-cut, the corset pushing her breasts high, the nipples barely covered. She felt Lucifer's arm holding her lightly as they danced, and their gloved hands meeting discreetly. Nothing could have been more proper.

'You're enjoying this?' he asked, beautiful mouth lifting at the corners. His touch burned and her blood raced.

'Very much.' It was all she could manage to reply.

'A trifle slow, don't you think?'

Her gown vanished. She was naked, and so was he, apart from a brocade robe with a sable collar. It was open down the front and his seemingly permanent erection jutted forth. The sedate music changed to a wild tempo. The dancers whirled and stamped, while some fell to the floor copulating, males with females, women with women, men with men. Others clustered in groups, taking their pleasure where they could. Some surrounded a ring in which two girls rolled in thick brown mud, tearing at each other's clothes and slapping at each other as they squirmed and wriggled. Elsewhere women bent over and were caned from behind while with their mouths they worshipped massive cocks presented to their lips. Others were stretched on racks underneath men who fucked them without mercy. The air was thick with the scent of arousal and cries of orgasm mingled with whimpers of diabolic pleasure. Everywhere, it seemed, flesh strained and muscles writhed in dark pleasure and through it all massively endowed satyrs strode, dispensing lashes with whips, strokes of wickedly pliable canes and resounding blows with their huge, hairy palms. Their magnificently erect phalli wagged before them and occasionally a woman would drop to her knees before one, who would stop and allow himself to be pleasured by her soft lips closing about the giant shaft and glans.

Curtains parted at one side of the room, showing a stage. An X-shaped cross dominated the centre, and a lovely young woman hung there, arms and legs tethered. A hairy satyr was wielding a many thronged whip, the lashes marking her fair skin with scarlet welts. She cried out piteously, and the creature bent and sucked her nipples, then his large fingers poked into her cleft, and he was encouraged by an eager audience. Her cries changed to whimpers of pleasure and she worked her clit against the goat-man's hand.

'You see?' Lucifer murmured in Kirsty's ear. 'He is not her ideal lover, but lust reigns supreme. She needs to come, and he is there, ready and eager. The whip has excited her, too. Look, he's impaling her on his dick. Do you mean to tell me that "love", as you call it, would make her climax more intense?'

Kirsty's loins were throbbing as she watched the couple. All around her creatures were engaged in sex, twosomes, threesomes, it didn't matter how many. The air was redolent with it, and it affected her, too. Maybe Lucifer was right and she deceived herself by thinking there was more to it. She saw Aphrodite in the arms of three gladiators, mighty armoured males who were acting out the game of rape. Cocks at the ready, they held her down and took their turn. She was yelling with delight.

But then, she's Lilith's daughter and a demon. I'm human and my values are different. Kirsty was trying to convince herself, fighting the raging heat pervading her entire body.

'Crap,' Lucifer whispered, his breath tickling her ear and sending shudders through her.

'It isn't crap.' She was angry at his assumption that what she felt for Dirk was nothing more than lust. 'I loved Martin, and now I feel the same for Dirk.'

'Show me. Let me share this emotion that seems to mean so much to you humans.' There was unappeasable hunger in his eyes. 'Do this, and share that love with me, and I'll speak to Michael for you. It will be a small price to pay for a lifetime of bliss with your beloved, won't it?'

'How can I love you... evil incarnate?'

'Evil is the food of genius. It's all done by mirrors, my dear, a great illusion.'

'It seems real enough to me.'

More and more examples of lechery and wantonness swirled around her, and it seemed that the pits of the Inferno opened, the screams of the tortured mingling with the cries of pleasure amid that ever-changing panorama of depravity. Aphrodite was in her element. She prised Kirsty away from Lucifer, and handed her to the rugged gladiators who threw her to the floor. She was pinned down, flat on her back, with them looming over her, naked cocks enlarged and eager.

'No!' Kirsty shouted, guessing their intention. 'Lucifer, make them stop!'

Great gales of laughter burst from him, as he grew and grew, giant-sized and omnipotent. 'I want to watch!' he bellowed, hands on hips, legs spread, shouting to his cohorts. 'Do you see this woman? She wants to save The Flying Dutchman!' Roars of vicious laughter greeted this, and he continued, 'He's mine, as you all know, but I may be lenient, proving that I, too, can be just and merciful, and that Him up there is not the only one.'

More laughter, cat-calls and whistles, shouts of advice and ribald suggestions. Kirsty was helpless. If Lucifer refused to aid her, then no one would. Why did I come to this terrible place? She asked herself and the answer came back, a soft whisper from Gabriel, 'To save the man you love.'

This was true and Kirsty took comfort from it. There was nothing she wouldn't do to bring this about. One of the gladiators knelt over her, his engorged prick ready for penetration. His mates held her arms and Aphrodite kicked her legs apart. Lucifer watched with glowing, scarlet eyes, fondling his genitals. The breath was knocked out of Kirsty as the man thrust into her brutally. He took his time, having already shot his spunk into Aphrodite not long before.

'Hurry up, you bastard!' Kirsty urged through gritted teeth.

His companions laughed and pushed their cocks into her captured palms, while Aphrodite handled her own breasts and rubbed her clit, excited by the spectacle. The man plunged and worked, seeking his satisfaction and at last completed the act. He withdrew and another took his place, but not before Kirsty had been rolled over and forced to kneel, her buttocks presented. She glared up at Lucifer, and his eyes flashed with something that resembled envy. He knocked her assailant out of the way and took his place. Even though he had assumed is usual stature, his weapon was large, and she was not accustomed to arse-fucking. His fingers scooped her juice out from her vagina and rubbed it into her anus. But even so her virgin sphincters put up stout resistance to the demon cock. The pain was immense and she went on screaming even as the muscles finally ceded to him and she felt his shaft begin to move in her most intimate tracts. She clung to the thought, *Dirk! Dirk! My one true love!* And endured the Devil's embrace.

There was no pleasure for her, only pain, and she collapsed forwards, trying to shake him off as soon as he had come. She stood up and the contempt she felt for him, for *all* of them, Dukes and Earls of Hell though they might be, shone in her eyes.

'Is that all you can do?' The rage in her voice gave them pause. Even Lucifer was quiet.

Then, 'What do you mean?' he growled.

She clung to her convictions. 'Life without love is no life at all.'

Her words brought an instant hush, then some of those in the background started to weep and wail and the lissom girls chained to the marble pillars, bowed their leads and sobbed. Even Aphrodite seemed deflated, though tried to brazen it out. 'Sentimental bollocks! It doesn't work here, baby!'

'Be silent, bitch!' The earth shook with Lucifer's fury. It split open in several places, sulphurous fumes rising in gusts, as from the heart of an active volcano. With them came unhappy spirits, writhing in grief, begging forgiveness.

Lucifer dismissed them curtly, having seen so many during his reign as Lord of the Underworld. Wearied of the scene, he suddenly caught Kirsty in his strong arms, unfurled his black wings, and shot up among the galaxies. Stars twinkled, universes flashed past, a thousand suns came into being, glowed, burned bright, then were extinguished. It was as if she was being granted a glimpse of creation, its progress, expansion and possible end.

Lucifer was no longer alarming, any more than Gabriel. Kirsty was strangely calm, accepting that she was privileged, seeing things that philosophers, poets and priests would have died to witness. *Why me?* She asked, and back came the words of the song, '*All you need is love. Love is all you need*'.

He was absorbed in a black hole, and then came to rest in a tropical paradise. Another illusion, no doubt, but just for that space in time, a reality of palm trees, a sandy shore and gently undulating blue sea. He set her down and assumed his Lucian image. He was wearing close-fitting white shorts and a T-shirt, suntanned and oh, so handsome. They were standing on the veranda of a beach-house and Kirsty wore a sarong over a bikini. A dark-skinned servant brought cocktails out to them, and it rather resembled a film-set. The drink was strong and she could feel herself losing control.

'Care for a swim?' Lucifer asked, and at once they were in the water, deliciously warm yet refreshing and he was submerged beneath her, his hands on her thighs, agile fingers finding her pleasure centre and stroking it gently.

There was nothing to remind her of who he really was. She was rapidly forgetting her reason for being there. Now it seemed a lovely episode with a skilled lover. He surfaced beside her, flinging back his long hair, his eyelashes spiky with water. She no longer feared him, resting her hands on his wet shoulders as they stood in the shallows.

'You could stay here with me forever, never aging or losing your beauty,' he whispered.

'Why do you want me?' Pity rose up in her, and she wondered how she could feel this for such a powerful individual who was steeped in wickedness.

'I don't know. Maybe you could save me. I am weary of my role. Your world doesn't need me so much. It is running on self-generating wickedness, an unstoppable course of destruction. Every kind of evil and depravity is in existence. It makes me dispensable.'

'Sweet-talking devil,' she said. 'I don't believe a word f it. You're trying to get my sympathy. And what a bribe? The opportunity to redeem Satan. Every woman's fantasy to save the bad boy and no one is more wicked than you.'

He was succeeding in blinding her, acting the English gentleman, courteous, amusing, even while treading water. 'Let me make love to you.' His voice was a sibilant hiss in her ear. Kirsty was reminded of the serpent in the Garden of Eden, and he was impossible to resist.

'I thought you'd done so, back at the orgy.' She was playing for time.

'Did you really think that uncouth lout was me?' He expressed dismay.

'Wasn't it?' His skin was so smooth under her hands, his eyes shining with sincerity.

'One of my less pleasant aspects. I have many names, many guises, but which one is really me?' He drew her up and, arm in arm, they made their way back to the beach-house. He spread towels on the veranda in the sun, arranged cushions under her head and stretched out beside her. She shaded her eyes against the brightness and, looking at him, thought that it was Dirk with her. Her heart opened to him and so did every part of her. He caressed her, wringing moans of pleasure from her lips, his hands masterful yet wonderfully gentle. Every move was perfect, each sequence like a well choreographed ballet, yet at the same time seeming spontaneous. He was casting a spell over her, but—

'I don't want to resort to magic tricks.' There was a wealth of sadness in his voice. 'Love me, Kirsty, love me, love Lucifer, the Son of the Morning.'

Things were spinning out of control. Kirsty was whirled up, laid across his outstretched arms while he bent his head and fondled her labia and clit with his full lips and agile tongue-tip. She was lost in sensation, rising to meet her orgasm, no longer knowing or caring who was bringing her to the point of no return - Dirk or Lucifer. She loved whoever was giving her this mighty, soul and body shattering sensation.

'I love you! I love you!' She yelled, and the words seemed to resound through time and space.

Losing consciousness, blackness engulfed her, and dimly, far away, she was aware of a phallus driving into her depths.

Gina was restless. She got up, left Seth sleeping and went into the galley, lit the gas, put on the kettle and waited for it to boil. She lifted down a mug, found the milk in the fridge, the sugar canister and teabags. For some unexplained reason, she couldn't get Kirsty out of her mind, almost deciding to head a posse to search the manor.

'She'd bloody kill me,' she muttered aloud. 'And so would I if anyone started messing with my love-life.'

Even so, she couldn't shake off the feeling of unease.

Never one for deep thought or contemplation of the whys and wherefores, she was nonetheless anxious, having a most uneasy feeling concerning Dirk and his handsome blond friend. There was something creepy about them, unlike Seth who was transparent as glass. She was getting fond of him and seriously considering settling down in this cosy Cornish hamlet, running her business, living with him and maybe starting a family.

What's up with me? I must be getting old, she thought, but not unhappily.

If only she could feel so calm about Kirsty.

She took two mugs into the main cabin and got into bed with Seth. He stirred sleepily, his hair tousled, as warm as a child, yet with the desires of a man. Gina sat beside him and sipped her tea.

'It's too damn early. Go back to sleep,' he grumbled, cuddling up to her.

'Will you come to Rosewood Manor with me in the morning?' She refused to be deflected from her purpose. 'I'll go with you to hell and back,' he promised, eyes tight shut.

It suddenly occurred to her that he might not be far wrong, and she mocked herself for being fanciful. Dirk was simply an eccentric millionaire, and so was Lucian. She put down her cup and clung to Seth, having him screw her, sleep forgotten.

Kirsty found herself at the side of the main road. It wasn't yet day, though the sky was lightening in the east and birds were chirping. She felt battered, bruised and confused. Where was she and how had she come to be there? Vague, alarming images floated in her mind. A giant owl? A crystal city? Lucian master of all? Then, gradually, the memories became clearer and she didn't want to know them! What had she done? What had she promised in return for Dirk's life and her own?

She started to walk, a signpost directing her to Lanyon Bray. With every step she took remembrance became clearer. Lucian was Satan, Lucifer, the Devil. Aphrodite was a Lilam, one of the demon daughters of Lilith, and Kirsty had gone to Hell in order to bargain with Lucifer. He wanted her to love him. Had she succeeded in convincing him of this? Would he now speak with the great angel, Michael, on her behalf?

It was several miles to Tregaskis Cottage, and that's where she determined to go. It was *hers*. Her bolt-hole and she needed its peace and seclusion as never before. Gina would be there, of course, unless she had spent the night with Seth, and that was more than likely, but Kirsty wanted to think things through and decide what to do next.

She became aware of a sound in the distance behind her, and turned to see headlights and the bulk of a long-distance lorry. A lift would be good, so she stuck out her thumb. The vehicle braked and a man leaned from the driver's window.

'Are you going near Lanyon Bray?' she asked.

'Sure. Hop up.' He opened the passenger door and held out a hand.

His grip was firm and strong, the palm warm and dry. She caught a glimpse of him in the interior light. He was young, with tousled brown hair, a pleasing face and humorous blue eyes. Suddenly, Kirsty felt the overwhelming urge to have an uncomplicated shag, something quick, a one-off with no strings.

'You've been driving long?' she asked as the lorry rolled.

'Since midnight.' He glanced at her in the driving mirror and grinned. 'Looks like you've been out on the own. Pub crawling or at a party or something?'

'You could say that.' Kirsty glanced at his left hand, resting lightly on his denim-covered thigh. She wanted to cover it with her own.

'Were you successful? I'll bet the guys are lining up to give you a seeing-to.'

He was brash and over-confident, but very, very *real*, and she was tired of demons and myths and legends. 'Maybe.' She shot him a flirtatious glance.

He paused, eyes on the road ahead, then, 'Could you do with a little bit more?'

It was now or never. 'Yes,' she said.

He gulped and she guessed that in spite of his brashness, he was surprised by her answer. 'OK, lady, I'm your boy.' And he turned into a lay-by, switched off the engine and took her into his arms.

He smelt of cheap aftershave and sweat. Cap off now, she ran her fingers through his spiky hair. He was certainly young and, despite his big talk, inexperienced. His kisses were wet, persistent and exciting. He put his hand into her bra and caressed her breasts. Human fingers, human warmth. It was delightful. He sighed, his erection starting to swell.

'Let's get into the back. I've a bunk there and sleep overnight sometimes.'

She had heard of this arrangement among long distance lorry drivers, and was intrigued to climb into the small area assigned for sleeping, complete with a telly and a bunk bed. He didn't rush her, and they lay there together, dawn light creeping through the small windows. She didn't want to know anything about him, not even his name, and it seemed that he felt the same. Whatever had taken place during her stay to Hell, something had changed, deep inside her.

They didn't even need to undress fully. She pushed up her top and lifted her skirt, he unzipped his jeans. Seeing that he was eager to take possession of her cunt and shoot his load, Kirsty made him wait, showing him how to excite her. It seemed he knew nothing about the clitoris, but became intrigued as he watched her stimulating the little organ and telling him how to do so, too.

'Spit on your fingers,' she said, demonstrating. 'Then rub my bud... like this...'

'No one's ever asked me to do that before.' He watched her wonderingly.

'I tell you, boy-o, get this off to perfection and the girls will love you for it.' She was breathing rapidly, roused by teaching him the art of female gratification.

'I thought that they wanted a cock in them and came off when I did. It's great watching you do that, makes me real horny.'

'You do it for me, and you'll enjoy it even more.'

'Like this?' He was hoarse with excitement, as she allowed him to stroke her cleft and hone in on her clit. His obvious arousal made her throb, nipples peaking, love-juice flowing.

Maybe this is how mating should be? She mused dreamily, feeling the warmth of his exploratory fingers. A quick coupling, done in the right way, of course, not a fumble when the woman remains unsatisfied, but without all the sentimental flim-flam associated with it.

She surrendered herself to pure sensation, an animal needing sexual relief. When she came, she let him know, yelling, 'That's it! Yes, yes, yes!'

He positioned himself on top of her and drove his cock home. He was well-endowed and her inner muscles clenched around his organ while the final spasms of orgasm shook her.

He slumped down with a sigh. She wriggled out from under him, eager to be on her way, the experiment over. That is what it had been for her, a test of what she was prepared to do. She pulled up her panties and rearranged her dress.

He seemed surprised that she had no desire to linger, or try to get a promise of further meetings out of him. He drove her to the bottom of the road leading to her cottage and there she kissed him lightly on the cheek and said goodbye, amused to think that he had no idea that her last lover had been Satan.

Dirk had never known such a dreamless sleep. He put it down to the knowledge that Kirsty loved him. He woke to find her gone and Lucifer standing in the window embrasure, watching him. A strange ambience hung around him, and Dirk stared at him suspiciously. Was he about to spring some unpleasant surprise? He reached for his robe and left the bed. Barend had brought him a cup of coffee that steamed on the nightstand.

'Don't bother about me,' Lucifer said pettishly.

'Oh, for God's sake! You can be so childish sometimes!' Dirk clicked his fingers and Barend appeared with another cup.

'Do you have to mention my adversary?' Lucifer accepted it, and lit a cigarette. 'And aren't you just the teeniest bit curious about how I got on with Kirsty?'

Dirk immediately alerted, worried about her. What had that smarmy devil done? 'Where is she?'

'Quite safe, dear boy. In her bed at Tregaskis Cottage, after fucking the lorry driver who gave her a lift home.'

'What are you talking about?' Dirk wanted to smash his fist into that mocking face.

Lucifer laughed. 'Calm down and listen to my good news. She visited me in Hell, brought by dear Aphrodite in her role as a night-hag. Such a helpful demon. And, for services rendered, I am prepared to consult with Michael. Yes, she's an entertaining bedfellow, your Kirsty. Not only that, she is teaching me what love means. Were it allowed by Himself, I might even become a reformed devil, but He won't let that happen. Who could He blame for all the ills of the world if it wasn't me? He might have to take the responsibility Himself.'

'I don't want to listen to all this. Just tell me, are she and I going to die together and find peace?'

'I hope to do better than that. The ball is in Michael's court now. You should be grateful.'

'How can I believe a word you say, Prince of Lies?' Hope flared in Dirk's heart, but he had learned to be cautious where Lucifer was concerned. Too often in the past, had he thought to have found the woman who would save him. Why should Lucifer relent now?

His tormentor, sometime companion, owner of his soul, rose to his impressive height and said, 'Kirsty is a most unusual person. She doesn't fear me or find me repulsive. We made love. Yes, I call it that deservedly, not lust, and though you have Her heart, she could spare a fraction of human tenderness for me. If Michael agrees, and I can't promise anything as he's full of his own importance and a touchy beggar, then you'll live out your lives on earth, marry, have children, and die at your allotted span. How does that suit you?'

'Why are you being magnanimous?' It was too good to be true.

Lucifer shrugged. 'I really don't know. A whim, perhaps. It's a novelty to do something noble, and I do make one or two stipulations.'

'I thought you might.' Dirk wondered what was coming next.

'I don't want to lose touch with you, or her. When the mood takes me, we shall board the ship, all three of us, with maybe one of your children, and ride the storm as we have done so often in the past. And, when I'm feeling lonely and despondent, Kirsty will comfort me in whatever way I fancy. Is that agreed?'

'There's always a catch in it with you, isn't there?' The idea of Kirsty coupling with the Devil was repulsive, yet there was no other way. There was always the chance that, in time, he would stop playing with them and leave them alone.

'I wouldn't be where I am today if I hadn't kept my wits about me and an eye on the main chance. Do you agree?'

Dirk hesitated for a fraction of time. Lucifer took him to Kirsty's bedside where she slept in the cottage. She lay there, and he caught his breath at her beauty. Her hair was spread on the pillow and her hand rested against her cheek, the quilt drawn up under her chin. No matter that she had coupled with Lucifer and the driver, there was an unspoilt innocence about her, kindness and goodness emanating from her soul.

If he could have her for a further fifty years, live with her, cherish her, then the bargain would be worth it. He took one of her curls and lifted it to his lips. The hair smelled of honeysuckle and he lost his last doubt.

'All right,' he said to Lucifer who stood there watching, a wistful smile touching his lips. 'I agree to your terms. See Michael and do what you can for us.'

Chapter Nine

Gina called in at the shop on the off-chance that Kirsty would be there. It was open, and Meg busy dusting. Everything looked as normal as could be.

'Is Kirsty here?' Gina tried to sound unfazed.

'She's out the back.'

Gina went into the yard and was pleased to see Kirsty acting so normally, hefting a cardboard box from the boot of her car. 'Are you OK?'

'Why shouldn't I be?'

Is it my imagination or is she a shade defensive? Gina found it hard to decide, but helped her in with goods bought from a recent auction in the local saleroom.

'I went to Seth's boat,' she went on. 'In fact, I spent the night there. Did you see Dirk?'

'I did.'

'And?' Gina didn't like the way Kirsty was avoiding her eyes.

'And everything is cool.'

It was like pushing a boulder up hill. 'Are you still marrying Robert?'

'That has to be sorted.'

'So you're not?'

Kirsty rounded on her. 'Give me a break, Gina. I've a lot on my mind.'

'OK, OK. Don't blow a fuse! I'm only trying to help.'

Kirsty cooled down, perching herself on the top of a crate and sighing. 'Sorry, but if I told you what really happened, you'd never believe it.'

'Try me.'

How can I do it? Kirsty thought. *In the broad light of day I can't really believe it* happened, let alone tell a friend! As for my disgraceful behaviour with the lorry driver! *Good Grief!*

Gina had lit up a cigarette and was looking at her expectantly. Kirsty decided to try. 'Well, for a start, are you going to accept the fact that neither Dirk nor Lucian is human?'

'You're right. I'm not. What d'you take me for? One of those air-heads who think there are fairies at the bottom of the garden, ghosts and goblins and things that go bump in the night?'

Kirsty flung her arms wide in exasperation. 'I told you that it was no use.'

'Oh, come on. What are you playing at?'

'I'm speaking the truth. You said there was something weird about them. There is.'

'I didn't mean really weird, like in supernatural. Just odd.'

'Oh, they're odd, sure enough. Dirk is The Flying Dutchman and Lucian is the Devil.'

'And I'm your Fairy Godmother! I don't think. Stop messing about, Kirsty. You may find it funny, but I don't.'

'I wish it was a joke, but it's true. The man I love will be condemned to wandering for ever if I don't save him.'

Gina's finely arched brows drew down in a frown. 'You're serious, aren't you?'

'Too right I'm serious. Would I make up a thing like that?'

Slowly stubbing out her cigarette in an antique brass ashtray, Gina gave her a steady stare. 'OK, you'd better try me. I'm all ears.'

'Not here. Let's go for a drive along the coast road.'

Kirsty stuck her head round the door into the shop, and gave Meg instructions, then went to her car, with Gina following and asking, 'Are we going to see Dirk?'

'Maybe later.' Kirsty drove in silence and pulled up in a parking space reserved for those who sought ocean views. This one was spectacular. They sat in silence for a moment, taking in the breathtakingly beautiful scene. Billowing waves stretched from the blue horizon, and rugged, volcanic rocks tumbled down to where the sea crashed against their roots that stretched towards the earth's core.

'It's certainly great. Makes you glad to be British,' Gina commented, leaning her head back against the seat, the sun beaming down on her face. 'Well, come on. Dish the dirt.'

Kirsty could hardly believe it herself, there in broad daylight, but she began by saying, 'The first time I saw Dirk I knew there was something special about him,' and she proceeded to relate every last detail of what had taken place, up to and including screwing the lorry driver.

Gina made no comment for a moment after she had finished, then, 'So you bonked the Devil? Made a pact with him, and he's off to see the Archangel Michael on your behalf? The man you're besotted with is none other than the legendary captain who roams the Seven Seas, seeking redemption through the love of a good woman, namely you?'

'That's about it, yes.'

'If I didn't know you better, I'd be asking about your medication.'

'So you believe me?' It was terribly important to Kirsty that she did. Never had she felt more alone.

'I'll need more proof.' Gina sounded dubious.

'We'll go and see Dirk, right now.'

Gina shivered. 'I'm not sure that I want to. Will Lucian.. Lucifer... be there?'

'Possibly. No need to fear him, Gina. Haven't you always liked rogues and vagabonds?'

'Only in fantasy like most red-blooded females, but not the real thing.'

Dirk sensed that she was coming. He had been restless all morning. Lucifer had gone on his mission to see Michael and Dirk couldn't quite understand his reasoning and why he was being lenient. He had learned not to trust a word he said. Once again he repeated the old adage, '*Who sups with the Devil needs a long spoon*'.

Barend moved about quietly in the background, organising the cleaning women who came up from the port. They always glanced sideways at the butler-cum-housekeeper and Dirk and his odd friends, but it gave them a wonderful source of gossip, as well as generous pay packets. Dirk's every wish was catered for as soon as he thought it, for Barend was immortal, too, and enjoyed it. He had no desire to do other than continue into eternity.

Where was she? Why hadn't she returned? Was she already regretting the impulse? Dirk strode towards the headland, the wind battering him, whipping the long hair back from his face, pressing his shirt and jeans close to his muscular body. Then he saw her car below him, like a toy vehicle winding its way slowly towards the manor gates. He wished himself by her, and there he was, barring the way.

'How the hell did he do that?' Gina gasped.

Kirsty braked and opened the driver's door. Dirk folded his arms around her, pressing her head against his chest. 'Darling, you're back. Yes, yes, Lucifer's told me what's happened. He's gone to see Michael. Yes, I mind because he's had you, but no, I don't blame you and can only thank you from the depths of my soul because you are willing to do this for me.'

To be pressed close to his heart again made everything right. This was where she belonged, forever and always. If one was very, very lucky, one found a soul mate, one single person who meant all and everything and without whose love, life was no life at all. Call it Fate, karma, destiny, whatever, the only perfect peace was when one met the other half of oneself.

She had forgotten Gina, and it was Dirk who called attention to her. 'You have told your friend?'

'Yes.' Kirsty's face was muffled as she breathed in the closeness of him. Why did they have to bother with anything else?

Dirk looked into Gina's eyes over the top of Kirsty's head. 'You believe her?'

'She isn't a liar, and yes, I believe, though the story is very far-fetched.'

'Thank you for that, at any rate. And you will help us?'

'If I can, but there's not much a mortal like me can do faced with elementals and angels and all the rest of the shebang.'

'Oh, but there is, Gina. They are low on kindness and love and emotion. I'm only part functioning in these human traits for it has been so long since I was a man.'

'Can I stay with you, Dirk?' Kirsty raised her head to ask.

He rested his lips against her forehead. 'Not yet, sweetheart. Our future lies in Michael's hands. I won't let you die for me, so, if he refuses to be merciful, then we must part forever and you'll never see me again.'

'No! No!' Pain sliced through her heart and she felt as if she was bleeding inside.

'Go home now and wait. I shall be with you as soon as a decision has been reached. Look after her, Gina.'

Kirsty knew that she owed it to Robert to see him. He was managing on his own, but she visited him at least once a day. He must be wondering where she was. Gina sat beside her silently as they returned to Lanyon Bray. Then, 'I'll mind the shop while Meg does her lunch hour bar work. You get off and do your explaining to Robert. I shouldn't like to be in your shoes.'

'You *do* believe me now, don't you?'

'Well, I guess so, though it's pretty wild. See you later.'

Explaining to Robert was the last thing in the world Kirsty wanted to do. For the hundredth time she wished she'd never got involved with him. She'd been trying to run away from Dirk, using Robert as a pawn in a not very honourable game.

As she walked up the path through the graveyard to the converted chapel, she heard music coming from the opened windows of the living-room. It no longer awed her because it had once been God's house. She had learned a lot about Him lately, and the chapel held no fears for her. Robert hobbled to the door as she let herself in. He had given her a key, but she intended to return it to him.

'Darling, I've been trying to call you. Where have you been?'

'To Hell and back.' Her honest answer simply made him laugh. He thought she was joking.

'I've missed you so much.'

He was big and rugged and reassuring, everything she could have wanted in a man, but it just wouldn't do. He attempted to kiss her and guide her up the stairs to the gallery that gave on to the bedrooms, but she resisted.

'We must talk.' She sat on the couch and made him take the armchair opposite, refusing to be put off by his worried expression. 'I can't marry you, Robert.' She was holding the engagement ring in the palm of her hand. Now she opened it and the circle of diamonds fell on to the coffee table.

'What? Why?'

It was awful to see a man so crushed, but she continued remorselessly, knowing that if she stopped it would never be said. 'I'm not in love with you. I thought it wouldn't matter as we have such a lot in common, but it does.'

'There's someone else.' He brought this out as if he had feared it all along, unable to believe his good fortune.

'Yes.' This was more difficult than she would have dreamed possible.

'May I ask who it is?'

'Dirk Stratten.' Just to say his name thrilled her immeasurably. I'm like a schoolgirl with her first crush, she thought.

'I feared as much.' The rage in his voice frightened her. It's not wise to tamper with a strong man's feelings and she had hurt him.

'You don't understand...'

'Oh, yes, I do! He's rich, handsome, and younger than me...'

'It's not that. Let me explain. He's the Flying Dutchman and like Senta, the heroine of Wagner's opera, I have to save him.'

He stared at her as if she was mad, and then gave a cynical laugh. 'He's told you this, has he? What is it? A new chat-up line?'

'I know you'll find this hard to credit, but his friend, Lucian, is the Devil and made this bargain with him long ago. I can save him, but Dirk doesn't want me to die for him so Lucifer, that's Lucian's real name, has arranged to see the Archangel Michael in order that Dirk may be forgiven and we can be together until we die naturally.'

'Someone is pulling your leg.' Robert's face was dour. 'Or else you've made this up to let me down gently.'

She dropped to her knees beside him. 'I wouldn't do hat. I have too much respect for you. Dirk and I are waiting for Lucifer's return and, depending on what Michael has agreed, we shall take it from there. Whatever the result, Dirk doesn't want me to sacrifice myself for him. He will step out of my life and I'll never see him again.'

'Then there's hope for me, if this happens?' He lifted her up towards him between his legs, the plastered one straight and unwieldy.

She shook her head, wishing it were otherwise. 'That will be it. I shall never love again and wouldn't be so cruel as to pretend that I could make a life with you. I'm so sorry, Robert.'

She heard a sound from the stained-glass windows and knew that Dirk was listening. He was pleased.

And Lucifer? Where was he? Just for a flash, she caught sight of him in Michael's golden palace. Its dazzle hurt the astral eye. Both were dressed in royal robes and lounged on divans, ebony and ivory chess pieces set out on a chequered board. Nymphets and chubby cherubs brought in goblets of wine and cornucopia filled with fruit. Others plucked at heavenly instruments, producing glorious sounds. The two mighty angels were debating while they played and had not yet come to a conclusion or struck a bargain. Such weighty matters could not be hurried.

Robert heaved a sigh. 'I suppose it was too good to be true. But whether or not I believe your story is another matter. Why didn't you have the guts to say it was over, and have done with it?'

'Because I wanted you to know the truth. Dare I hope that we can still be friends?'

'I don't think so. This would be just too painful, but if ever you want an estate agent, then I'm your man.'

'Do you still employ that good-looking receptionist? I'll bet she'll be glad to see the back of me.' *I wish*, she thought, wanting to salve her conscience.

'Don't start matchmaking. I can fend for myself. I think you should leave now,' said Robert.

'Whew! What a day! You'll never believe what Kirsty told me!' Gina flopped down on the divan in Seth's living accommodation at the back of his workshop.

'Try me.' He wandered from the bathroom, a towel looped round his hips, all tanned, muscular, hairy man. She creamed her panties at the sight of him.

'You'll laugh.'

'That's better than crying, isn't it?' He disappeared into the kitchen and returned with two cans of lager, handing her one. Then, careless of the loosened towel, lowered himself down beside her. With an arm around her neck and the other hand holding the tin to his lips, 'Go on,' he said. 'Tell me all about it.'

'Do you believe in the legend of The Flying Dutchman?'

'Course I do. Doesn't every sailor?'

She sat up at this. 'You've seen him?'

He nodded. 'And his ship. I was deep-sea fishing once with my Dad and a terrible storm sprang up out of nowhere and there it was, an old-fashioned sailing boat and he was at the wheel and his crew were like skeletons and Old Nick himself clung to the rigging, laughing fit to bust.'

She gripped him by the arm. 'You're not making this up, are you?'

'No. Dad told me who it was and how he got to be there and he said he'd seen him before, when he was in the navy during the Second World War, and how all the blokes were scared stiff, but some said it was lucky to see him, and that he was looking for a woman who'd love him so much that she'd die for him.'

'That's what Kirsty said.' Gina sat back, drank her beer and recounted Kirsty's story. By the time she had finished he was enthusiastic, believing every word. 'So that's the geezer that threw the party and his friend was Satan? Wow!'

'Keep it to yourself. No blabbing to your surfing buddies. We've got to think of Kirsty.'

'I'll be silent as the grave,' he promised, and his big, weathered hands started an exploration of her body, divesting her of her clothes till she wore nothing but her lacy panties.

The towel had been kicked aside and he lifted her to her feet, walking her to the back of the couch, kissing her all the way. She bent over the plush upholstery, feeling it squash against her bare breasts, belly and upper thighs. Seth's hand was cupping her mound, his middle digit parting her crack and massaging her clitoris. He was a country boy, not a sophisticated townie, yet he knew precisely what buttons to press in order to pleasure a woman. He could be gentle and persuasive or tough and forceful, but the outcome would be the same, orgasms for both of them - her first and then him, no disappointment or let-down.

He lifted her hair away and nibbled the nape of her neck, murmuring, 'Are you enjoying that, my lovely?'

His erect cock was pressing against her bottom crack, seeking the entrance to her love-channel. This was his preferred route to bliss, though he would sometimes, playfully, try out her anus, but usually ended up in her cunt. She loved being naked and yielding to his strength. Boys like Craig were all very well, but it took a mature man to fully satisfy an experienced woman like her. He seemed to know what she wanted, when she wanted it. Her nipples were chaffed by the leather. His hand came round to palpate them. Her pussy craved attention. He fulfilled the need. She yearned to feel his cock ramming into her. He did just that. Her clitoris was throbbing. He did not stop rubbing it. She was coming, yelling, swept into a shattering climax. He speeded up his thrusts and came a second after.

She slumped down, and he rested against her. There was no rough withdrawal. He let her take her time, though supporting his weight. Slowly, carefully, he pulled out, and she turned, linking her arms around his neck, feeling as if every bone in her body had dissolved in pleasure.

'We're good together, you and I. Make an ace team.' He wasn't pressurizing her or demanding a commitment, but she was inclined to give it anyway.

With his support, she was finding it easier to come to terms with Kirsty's outlandish tale. He was a man who had his feet very firmly planted in the soil, yet he believed in The Flying Dutchman. There was no question about it in his mind.

He fetched more beer, padding around mother-naked. 'So, what's she going to do about it?' he asked, continuing the conversation that had been interrupted by sex.

'I told you. She's hoping that Michael will consent to let her marry Dirk and live happily ever after.'

He cuddled up against her on the couch. 'There's bound to be a price, isn't there? You don't get anything for nothing, especially when you're dealing with elementals. Anyway, it would be a pity if we sailors couldn't be on the lookout for the doomed captain and his crew when the weather's bad and there's a storm brewing. Sort of keeps us on our toes, and is a great way of getting drinks bought us when we tell about it in the pub. Is there any chance of meeting him again? That party he gave was a blast.'

'I don't know, but I'll see what I can do. You must promise not to shag Aphrodite or any of her sisters.'

'Would I, when I've got you, babe?'

She half believed him, but wasn't taking any chances, playing with his cock again, making it stand firm. Seth would find that she, all woman, would be quite enough or him.

This is unsatisfactory, Lucifer thought, brooding over the chessboard. Why do I still have to take second place to these sycophantic angels who toadied to God, while His favourite, me, was cast into the Abyss?

It still rankles, even after all these eons.

'Rise above it,' suggested Michael, reading him like an open book. 'In a way, I envy you. At least you are your own man. I have to do what He wants.'

'Oh, I'm familiar with all the arguments.' Lucifer was in the frame of mind to bicker. Kirsty had disturbed him, and now this meeting with an angel who liked to think himself superior had rubbed salt in the wound.

'A fine lady, I agree.' Michael had discarded his armour for a robe, but it was to hand, with a squire alert to help him don it, if need arose. There might be a dragon who must be slain, an army seeking a fiery leader, wrongs to be righted. He bore all the aspects of a stern, fearless, military man. 'There's no rest for the angelic,' he remarked with a smile.

'She's sincere, I'll grant you that.' Lucifer's mind wasn't on the game and let himself be cornered, putting his queen in check.

Michael shrugged. '"Love laughs at locksmiths."'

'Meaning what, exactly?'

'It is the greatest power there is. You know that, and so do I.'

'But can we break rules for it?'

Michael rose to his full, impressive height. A fine figure of an angel. Although the squire had not appeared to move, the mighty warrior was now fully clad in chainmail, shield on one arm, sword in the other. His flowing hair cascaded from beneath a helmet, and his perfect face shone. 'We'll consult the Akashic Record. There is obviously some strong link between these two souls.'

At once they stood on the far reaches of the universe, examining the great rainbow that circled Earth, wherein was pictured every event that had ever happened there, and every single life ever lived. 'Not one life, but countless lives per soul,' Michael said. 'Marking their evolution, development and passage along the way to perfection. Once reached, it will never be necessary for them to return. They will become High Initiates, visiting other worlds, but not this vale of sorrow.'

'But we have to,' Lucifer pointed out.

'Of course. This is our part in the scheme of things. Even the Christ has to come back.'

'And the Buddha.'

'And the Prophet Mahomet and all other Holy Ones. Our task is to teach. Even yours, Lucifer, Son of the Morning.'

That's the trouble with Michael. He's just too logical and reasonable, though he can be stern, Lucifer thought, knowing full well that he could keep nothing from him.

They traced Dirk's and Kirsty's lives through the great Record, back and back, though she had been born more often, due to him being stuck in time. Before he came to earth as the Dutchman, their contacts had been many and varied. Sometimes he'd been female and she male, lovers, fathers and mothers, sisters, brothers. There was one outstanding link. In each life their love for one another had remained steadfast. And there had been a knowing and a recognition, no matter how strange the circumstances.

She had missed the other half of herself during the past three hundred years, though unaware why she felt that isolation and emptiness that nothing would alleviate. Whatever had happened to her recently had been a trifle compared to the loneliness. She had found a deep, inner peace since learning the truth, though troubled on the surface.

'There's been a thread of humanity throughout her incarnations.' Michael was studying her progress intently. 'And a rise in her spiritual awareness. Do you see? I'm not speaking of Christianity. It goes beyond that. In each of her lives she has helped those around her, be she a whore, a mercenary soldier, farmer, nurse. It doesn't matter what role she elected to play.'

'And it all led to this, being reunited with her soul mate?'

'That's what the Record tells us and it can't be changed, bent, warped or altered. It is Fate, for want of a better word.

'And what of Dirk?'

'A younger soul, impetuous, proud, very often highborn and not always acting unselfishly. He needs her to steady him and bring out his full potential.'

'So what is to be done, or if it is as you say, can we alter anything? What about his punishment?'

'I shall have to consult Gabriel and the others. Leave it with me, for you can't be present.'

Once again Lucifer was made to feel excluded and his face darkened, taking on the ugly visage associated with his devilish persona. 'Shall I never be forgiven? Surely my work here is almost completed? Man is sinful enough and doesn't need me. He has made his own hell on earth.'

'That is not for you or me to decide. It is your pride talking again, the arrogance that had you banished from heaven in the first place. Go away, Lucifer. I will be in touch.'

In a rage so violent that it raised a hurricane, making the seas boil and the winds uproot trees and smash buildings, Lucifer crashed through the world and entered his own domain.

His minions cringed, and he strode through his palace, kicking them aside, lashing out with his bull-whip and shouting for Aphrodite. She came, gliding gracefully, at once alert for trouble and prepared to soothe her master's savage breast.

'What is it, sire?' she crooned, while her sisters appeared in various seductive guises.

They writhed around the furious angel, willing to do anything he desired.

He slumped in his throne on a dais, wreaking his fury on everyone. The nubile twins did their best to please him, one sucking his cock, the other teasing his nipples, but he cast them roughly aside. Women screamed in terror as they were pursued by warriors intent on rape. Lucifer's cock refused to harden. He was bored, bored, bored! He damned Kirsty and Dirk, but how could he damn them when he himself was damnation? He was thwarted on every side.

The wall slid open revealing one of his torture chambers. It was bathed in crimson flame and the occupants were not only condemned to suffer endless pain, but endless pleasure, too. Aphrodite took her flogger to a beautiful creature who had been a queen in her earthly life. Now she hung on a cross, vulnerable and helpless to prevent whoever desired from touching her breasts and genitalia. One of her handsome lovers who had helped her corrupt her court, was strapped across a wooden vaulting horse, while satyrs, monks and wild creatures plundered his anus. He yelped with pain/pleasure while she was forced to watch.

In other areas, wild orgies took place where nothing was forbidden. There was almost too much freedom, taking away any sense of naughtiness. Every combination was used, and it was hard to see where one person started and another ended. There was a tangle if limbs, human and otherwise, grinning faces or those wreathed in ecstasy, animal masks, enormous phalli and ballooning breasts.

None of these spectacles brought any satisfaction to Lucifer. He missed Dirk and he missed Kirsty. Both had lifted the veil a fraction and he had glimpsed what human love and contact could be. Aphrodite wove her supple arms round his neck.

'Don't fret, master. It will pass, like everything else passes. You'll find a new companion to torment, if you lose Dirk. As for Kirsty? She is but a creature made up of water, mostly. Unlike us, who will continue for all time, beautiful, alluring and powerful. Would you really wish it to be otherwise?'

'It doesn't matter what I wish,' he grumbled sullenly, tugging at the gold chain that linked the rings inserted in her pierced nipples.

She winced, then said, 'You're just feeling low. I'll bet the girls and I can make you feel better.'

In an instant a group of lissom young women were dancing, as supple as reeds blowing in the breeze. Veils undulated around their limbs as they moved gracefully, performing an erotic saraband during which they caressed each other's cracks and nipples. Their moans of pleasure rang sweetly in Lucifer's ears and his confidence returned, his cock rising, a great, burgeoning staff between his thighs.

Aphrodite clasped it, and the girls wove in and out, each one caressing that massive appendage as they passed. With cries and laughter, women swooped down from the sky, some riding the wind, others mounted on broomsticks. They were celebrating one of their seasonal solstices, when ritual magic was performed. They worshipped the Old Religion, but some practiced the Black Arts, spiteful ill-wishers. They had all come to pay homage to The Fallen One.

Their presence heartened him. He held his head high and assumed his most magnificent and handsome form. The women bowed down before him and every one of them wanted to feel that splendid tool buried deep in their bodies. Not only women. There were warlocks who worshipped him and others who without knowing it, had given themselves to him long ago under the guise of politicians or war-mongers.

Lucifer could feel himself hovering on the edge of a mighty orgasm. He closed his eyes and spurted and his followers bathed themselves in his spunk, crying his name aloud. What did two tiny people like Dirk and Kirsty or even a senior angel called Michael matter compared with this adulation?

Chapter Ten

How much longer do I have to wait? Kirsty felt she might explode with impatience. There had been no word from either Dirk or Lucifer. It was as if nothing had ever happened and easy to kid herself that she had come to Cornwall to set up a business, without the hint of an emotional entanglement.

If only! she thought, stressed out and weary. It was necessary for her to concentrate on establishing the shop. The Season was short and this was when money was to be made. So, with Gina's encouragement, she attended house clearances and auction sales, building up her stock. The area was rich in antiquities and attractive bric-a-brac, and cheaper than Bath, always a pricey district, famed for its collectable items.

When engaged in the cut and thrust of dealing, she was able to forget Dirk. Gina was an ideal companion, a tough cookie when it came to striking a bargain, and Kirsty was looking forward to her becoming established there, leaving Kelly in command at Bath. It seemed that her independent friend was softening towards Seth and maybe, just maybe, bells might chime for a double wedding. This was Kirsty's dream, though she didn't dare mention it.

Day followed day, and every night she went to bed alone. No telephone call, no message, nothing from Dirk. She feared the worst. Either he had decided that he didn't love her after all, or he was determined to go it alone, saving her life and removing himself from her existence. It did occur to her that Lucifer was stringing them along, having been given a decision but keeping them waiting out of pure mischief.

'Can you and Dirk be married in church?' Gina was shaking out a pair of magnificent brocade curtains that had gone under the hammer that morning. Newly cleaned and immaculate, she had bought them for a song.

She had a disconcerting habit of bringing forth this kind of statement without warning, and Kirsty was nonplussed for a moment, then, 'I haven't even thought about it,' she replied, though this wasn't quite true.

'Liar!' Gina chided. 'What woman worth her salt doesn't daydream of walking down the aisle on the arm of her beloved? I just wondered how you'd get on with a vicar, seeing as how Dirk is in league with the Devil. Can I be matron-of-honour?'

Kirsty faced her in exasperation, hands on her hips. 'Look, nothing has been decided. We don't even know if we can be together. As for a church wedding? I shouldn't think so. I'd be happy with a Civil Ceremony. And you aren't even married yourself so how can you be a matron-of-honour?'

'Stop splitting hairs,' Gina retorted.

'Why don't you go for a Handfasting ritual.' Meg dropped this into the conversation as she whisked through to fetch the order book. 'I'm sure Mr Caldecote would approve.'

Robert? Kirsty was glad that Meg had obviously got the wrong end of the stick 'What's that?'

Meg paused, then went on, 'It's an ages old marriage custom. I belong to the Goddess Temple and could put you in touch with the right people.'

'Sounds great,' Gina enthused. 'I've heard of it. A pagan thing, stone circles and Wicca and all that jazz. I'm up for it.'

'You're jumping the gun, Gina. Thank you, Meg, and I'll be in touch, but we can't even think about it yet.'

'OK. No hassle. My friends would be very willing to do it. Just let me know when,' and Meg returned to serving a customer.

'The suspense is killing me,' Gina complained. 'God knows what it's doing to you! Get on the blower and demand that Lucifer or Michael or whoever's in charge, makes up their fucking mind.'

At that moment Kirsty's mobile trilled, startling them. It was just too much of a coincidence. Their eyes met as Dirk's voice said, 'Can you come up right away, Kirsty? I've something to tell you.'

'Yes. Of course. What is it?'

'Just come,' and he switched off.

'So that's it. You and Michael made yourselves out to be very important, but it was ordained anyway. Neither of you could have changed a thing.' Dirk paced the poolside, while Lucifer reclined on a sun-lounger, a straw hat shading his eyes, his skin gleaming with protective lotion.

'Well, he might have known, but I wasn't sure until we looked at the Akashic Record.'

'Not quite so omnipotent as you thought you were, eh?' It pleased Dirk to bring him down a peg.

'There's no need to be like that. You've got what you wanted, haven't you? And my little proviso is a mere trifle. You may find it rather fun and a relief from the tedium of human existence.'

'I would prefer to have you out of my life forever.' Dirk gazed moodily over the water. Where was Kirsty? He couldn't wait for her to arrive.

'That's not very nice.'

'You're not very nice. Why can't you leave me alone?'

'I think you'd miss me. Who would you roll dice with?'

'I could get along without that.' Dirk gave a crooked smile, but the glance he threw the Devil was not entirely unfriendly. They had been together so long.

'Yes, yes, of course. You'll be able to play Scrabble or something equally stimulating with your lady wife, when you get bored with fucking her.'

Dirk's smile broadened. 'You know, one day you might say something halfway pleasant. It'll shock you, Lucifer.'

'I can't wait,' he jibed, then added, 'Get your cock out. Here she comes.'

Kirsty appeared, rounding the side of the house to the swimming area. Dirk wanted to sweep her into his arms and carry her to bed, but Lucifer's presence brought a measure of formality to the occasion. It must be a one-off in the annals of mankind and angels. Her eyes were searching for him, and her hands reached out. He took them in his.

'Oh, Dirk, tell me... tell me!' she begged.

Lucifer lounged to his feet, tanned and expensively groomed, wearing miniscule white shorts and elegant designer sunglasses. 'Shall I give her the news, Dirk? Or will you?' It was obvious that he wanted to be the bringer of important tidings.

'Don't keep me waiting.' She fixed her eyes on him, while clinging to Dirk's hand as if it were a lifeline.

'Very well. The Archangel Michael and I examined your progress on the Akashic Record where everything is filed, and the result appears to be that your destiny is already written. You are to save The Flying Dutchman, marry him and bear his children.'

Kirsty flung herself to her knees before Lucifer, clasping his bare brown legs. 'Oh, thank you! Thank you!'

'There's no need to over-do it, darling.' Dirk helped her to her feet. 'It wasn't his work, after all. It had been woven into the fabric of past, present and future and there was nothing he or Michael could have done to alter it.'

'Thank you for being there, anyway.' Kirsty was still looking at Lucifer, a searching look that seemed to contain something within it personal to the two of them. Despite having his arms around her, Dirk felt a pang of anxiety. The Devil was not going to be so easy to get rid of.

'Bless you, my children.' Lucifer assumed a beatific expression, hands steepled together piously. 'Alas, your union will not be celebrated in church. This would hardly be seemly, but I believe you already have some thoughts on the matter, haven't you, Kirsty?'

'Oh, yes.' Her face was so radiant that Dirk could hardly bear to look at her. 'A register office wedding in Lanyard Bray, and then a Handfasting ceremony in the open somewhere. You'd be able to come to that, wouldn't you, Lucifer?'

'I'd be honoured, but have a feeling that the Goddess Temple would not welcome me. I'll attend the reception, if I may.'

'Of course. So we can start planning? I'm hardly able to believe it's true.'

'You're very eager to get rid of me.' Lucifer assumed such a mournful expression that Dirk wanted to laugh.

'She's invited you to the reception. What more do you want?' Dirk wished he'd go away. He needed to be alone with Kirsty, to make love with her and convince himself that this wasn't just a wonderful dream.

'No more than my due.'

'And what is that?'

'Nothing stressful. Indulge your old ally. All will be revealed on your wedding night. Now, I'll leave you. No doubt you have much catching up to do. For my part, there's a conference of Government ministers I simply must attend. A Peace Treaty to be signed, my dears. What a farce!' And he was gone, though not before tweaking Kirsty's arse.

Dirk swung her up in his arms. 'It's true, darling! Wandering is over. I shall live with you and grow old with you, watch our children growing up, become a grandfather. And it's all because of you.'

'It hasn't really sunk in yet. I still can't really believe it. Oh, Dirk, there's so much to plan. Where shall we live?'

Her hair was spread over his arm, its perfume bewitching him. He wanted to possess her, pleasure her, and convince himself that this was real, not some rosy dream. It was hard to think of anything sensible.

'I have properties all over the world, but I like it at Rosewood. It's special because we met here. This could become our family home. I have so much wealth that there is no need for us to worry about finance. We can have the best of everything.' This bonus became suddenly apparent. He had taken it for granted before.

'This seems unfair when there are so many people who have nothing.'

'Then we can support charities. Whatever you think worthwhile.' He was willing to give her the moon and stars had she asked for them.

Still holding her, feather-light in his arms, he left the Great Hall, mounting the wide staircase and carrying her to the Master Bedchamber. There was so sign of Lucifer, the room filled with the glorious glow of afternoon sunshine. Dirk searched, using that special antenna that he had retained even though now mortal, but there was no sign of anyone demonic or even angelic.

He was now free to concentrate on Kirsty, laying her gently down and taking his place beside her. Soon it really would be his place when he became her legal husband and they were bound together in the Handfasting.

Her touch on his face and hair was soothing yet arousing. His cock started to swell, demanding entrance to her body. Dirk knew better than to yield to that one-pointed urge. Kirsty deserved to be wooed. He wanted to employ all his skill to bring her the greatest delight. She had not delayed to change for their meeting, still wearing blue jeans and a vest with shoe-strings straps. She kicked off her thong sandals and he helped her out of the denims. Her white panties and bra contrasted with her suntanned skin, and he sat back on his haunches and admired the perfection of her body.

This lovely female was his forever. It was not necessary that she die for him. He murmured a stanza from one of his favourite poets, '"The Moving Finger writes; and, having writ, Moves on: and all Thy piety nor Wit Shall lure it back to cancel half a Line, Nor all thy Tears wash out a Word of it".'

'That's by the Persian poet, Omar Khayyam,' she said. 'I love his stuff, and he lived so long ago, in the eleventh century. You and I have a lot in common, and will never come to the end of sharing and enjoying.'

'Starting here, beloved.' Dirk didn't want to speak any more and bending over, he closed her mouth with his.

It was honey-sweet, moist and yielding, her tongue joining his. As he kissed her, his hands moved over her breasts, feeling the nipples crimp beneath the bra. Then he slipped the straps down and unfastened the garment at the back. Lucifer had supplied him with many houris through the centuries, voluptuous courtesans or wondrous apparitions, but none had thrilled him like this creature made up of flesh and blood, bone and spirit. She was warm, loving, generous and kind, and she loved him beyond all else.

He trailed a finger from her breasts to her navel, and from there took a pathway to her mound, weaving through the curly blond floss and parting her lower lips. She stirred, moaned and raised her hips, pressing her nubbin against his touch. Dirk spread her thighs, and allowed himself the privilege of running his tongue-tip across her wet, pink petals and sucking the hard bud protruding between her lips.

She tasted heavenly, her female essence oceanic, assailing his nostrils and sweeping him to the point of release. He succeeded in restraining his orgasm, wanting this to last. He rimmed her anus, licked her inner thighs, caressed each erogenous zone, until she was gasping and urging him towards completion. Her hands cupped his balls, her fingers played with his shaft and circled his helm, her lips wrung extreme sensation from the brown, puckered discs of his nipples.

'Don't stop!' she urged fiercely. 'I want to come... now!'

He longed to see her attaining bliss and bent over, his face close to her open sex. The lips were dark pink and swollen, juice seeping from her vulva and her clitoris was hard and red, straining from its little cowl as if begging him to rub it. Afraid that she might think him too rough, he kept the organ slippery wet, smoothing his finger over it gently.

She grew impatient, astonishing him by grinding her pubis, urging him to apply pressure and working herself hard, till she suddenly stiffened and yelped and he felt her clit throb and her vaginal entrance convulse. This was the moment to enter her, and he thrust so hard that his cock-head butted her cervix and her muscles clamped around him. It was a glorious sensation and Dirk had never before experienced anything like it. He was loved. He was saved. He had found her at last. His libation rose overwhelmingly and emptied into her.

He remained there for a seemingly endless time that was no more than a minute in reality, and then he shifted, pulled the quilt over them and enfolded her in his arms, her head resting on his shoulder. He had never known such peace since he was a child, recalling how his mother in long-ago Holland, that land of dykes and windmills, had tucked him into bed and sung nursery rhymes. The remembrance made him want to weep for his lost innocence.

Kirsty stirred and asked, 'Can I stay with you?'

'What about your reputation?' He kissed her eyelids, cheeks and throat.

'You can't be serious?'

He wasn't exactly familiar with Cornish propriety, but wondered if anyone would bother if the unwed Miss Anderson slept with him. 'Not really, though the residents of Lanyon Bray do take an interest in the comings and goings of their neighbours.'

'I know. Meg is a prime example, a friendly girl, but with a nose for juicy items of gossip. It was her who told me about the Handfasting, though she had it fixed in her mind that I was going to tie the knot with Robert.'

'What will she say when she knows it's me?'

'She'll be pleased, I expect, keen to have her friends perform the ritual.'

'And Lucifer can't be present.'

'Apparently not. This surprises me. I would have thought he'd be welcomed by the followers of Wicca.'

'No, my love. They worship Nature and are not into Black Magic or Satanism. He'd get the cold shoulder from them.' Dirk was happy to reassure her, wanting no part in Lucifer's machinations.

It was as if a great weight had been lifted from him. Energy filled his every sinew and he hauled Kirsty up until she sat astride him, her wet cleft anointing his lower belly. Her eyes were like stars as she gazed at him adoringly, and he reached up and held her breasts in his hands, weighing each perfect orb. His phallus was hard again, nudging between her crack that was ready to receive it.

'We're going to be so happy,' he said. 'No ceaseless roving, no longing for love that isn't there.'

'And no Lucifer.' Then she added, 'Well, not very often.'

From the tail of his eye, Dirk caught a lurid flash and his extra sense told him that they were no longer alone. Defiantly, he shouted, 'That's right, Kirsty. No Lucifer and his gang!'

'How wrong you are, old boy,' Lucifer said, materialising at the foot of the bed, backed by Aphrodite and her sisters.

'I thought I'd got rid of you!' Dirk blazed with an anger that was fuelled by frustration.

'That's not very polite. What a way to greet a loyal friend.' Lucifer pulled an offended face, then leaned over and ran a hand up Kirsty's leg.

'Get away from her!' Dirk shouted, but he struggled in the embraces of Aphrodite and the other Lilim, Harlots of Hell, Succubae and Night Hags, all adept at rousing base desires. He had been on the point of another ejaculation with Kirsty, his cock hard and ready.

He fought against his response to their silken caresses, trying to reach Lucifer and prevent him from seducing Kirsty. His love was stronger than his lust, and he tore himself away from the demon women. Lucifer turned and grinned at him. At once he was seized by invisible hands, unable to move a muscle. Then Kirsty was tied to the posts of the tester bed, arms and legs stretched out, and her tormentor flexed his muscles and cracked a whip through the air. Dirk heard the impact and her strangled shriek as it landed on her naked back.

'Let her go!' he shouted. 'Do what you will with me, but don't hurt her!'

'Shut up, you weakling!' Lucifer was in his element, taking out his wrath on the woman who had stirred emotions in him which he would much rather not have experienced.

The whip rose and fell. Kirsty's cries were piteous. There was nothing Dirk could do to help her. Lucifer threw the whip aside when he had finished torturing her, then he had her tossed on the bed and drove his huge phallus into her bruised and battered body.

In the next instant he and his minions had gone, leaving Dirk and Kirsty as they had been before their arrival, about to make love again. There was not a single mark on her body. It was as if the incident had never taken place, but Dirk knew different.

'That's how he works, darling,' he said soothingly, trying to calm her fears. 'In spite of our help from the angels, he has a knack of getting his way.'

Gina helped Kirsty arrange everything, from the guest list to the Registrar to Meg's involvement with the Goddess Temple. True to her word, she had introduced Kirsty to her friends who were only too happy to organise the Handfasting.

The dress had to be made and, following instructions from Meg, she chose crimson, the colour of passion. It consisted of a basque bodice laced at the back and with a long, swirling skirt, red satin shoes, elbow length red gloves and a flower wreath to be worn on her unbound, flowing hair. A taffeta cloak of the same vibrant hue would drape her shoulders during the ritual. This was to be carried out in the circle of stones, known as the Seven Sisters, that had stood on the cliffs near Rosewood Manor since time immemorial.

Kirsty phoned her mother in New York and said without preamble, 'I'm getting married.'

'What a surprise! Is he someone nice? My goodness, do you want us to come over?'

It was great to hear that familiar voice and Kirsty forgot there had been an estrangement. 'I'd love you to. Dirk, that's the man I'm marrying, says not to worry about the fare. He'll pay for everything. He's rich, Mum. It's no problem.'

'Good. Well, I mean that's good for you. But there's no need for him to pay. Tony's doing very well indeed and I've gone back to dress designing. It's high time you met Peter. He's three now and I'm sure you'll love him. He's so cute.'

There was more of this, dates were exchanged and arrangements to get in touch when they were leaving so that a car could be hired and other essentials sorted. 'They don't need you to sponsor them. Tony's doing OK and Mum is picking up a lot of designer work,' Kirsty told Dirk later.

'And your father?'

Kirsty flinched. She didn't want to think about him. 'It will hurt Val, that's my Mum, if he and his tart are invited. Oh, dear... families! You should be grateful you don't have any.'

'Lucifer is my only "family", and he's not invited to either of the services, but whether he'll stay away or not is another matter entirely.' Dirk leaned over and brushed aside her hair so that he might kiss the back of her neck. It was hard for Kirsty to concentrate on writing invitation cards.

The phone bleeped and, 'Hello, darling girl,' a voice gushed, instantly recognizable as Andy's. 'Got your invite! What a surprise! Who is the lucky man? Do I know him? Is it formal? I'm dying to buy a new outfit. Yes, Alec will come. Try to keep him away, my dear! He loves a wedding. It always makes him cry. Maybe it will be us one day, and then I shan't have to sing, "Why am I always the bridesmaid, never the blushing bride?"'

'"No one loves a fairy when she's forty,"' Kirsty chimed in with the lines from another song.

'Oh, you bitch! That's not very friendly,' he squeaked, but she knew he was enjoying every moment of it.

The list was growing, on her side at any rate. Dirk invited no one, his wandering existence denying him relations or friends, but Kirsty's and Gina's acquaintances made up for this. The reception was to be held at Rosewood Manor, a sumptuous affair. The caterers had been booked, and a band for dancing. No expense had been spared. Lucifer was conspicuous by his absence, and Kirsty hoped that he had grown tired of playing games with them.

'What about a best man?' Gina asked Dirk when he called at the cottage to arrange a meeting with the priestess who was performing the Handfasting.

'I hadn't thought of that.'

He was looking windswept and interesting and Gina could see his attraction. He's indeed a sexy hunk, she thought, saying aloud, 'I'm not sure if it's strictly necessary, but I think Seth would do it. Why don't you ask him? Buy him a drink one night and mention it.'

'These customs are strange to me.' He seemed almost hesitant and shy.

She didn't find him easy to get on with and assumed it was because he had so odd a background. He seemed perfectly normal, apart from having those extraordinary film star good looks. Trust Kirsty to wind up with a weirdo, she sighed and set about persuading Seth that it would be a great idea if he was The Flying Dutchman's best man, to hold the ring, and make speeches and try to snog the bridesmaids. He didn't need much urging.

'Shall I become famous and part of the legend?'

'Maybe, but you'll keep your trap shut and don't talk to the press or I'll chop off your prick!' she threatened.

'You know you wouldn't do that, babe. It's much too valuable to you,' he smirked, pulling her back against him and letting her feel its length and girth through his jeans. 'When are we going to get married?'

'Have I agreed?' She was besotted with him, but not about to let him know it.

'Aw, you want to, don't you?'

'I'll think about it, but first I've got to see Kirsty through this. There's so much to do. You go and see Dirk and don't go all gaga because you know who he is. And keep it to yourself!'

'So, you've let him go?' Aphrodite strolled across the marble floor towards Lucifer. His handsome face was set in dark, moody lines.

She knew him too well to do anything to add to his annoyance, but could not resist teasing him a little. It was unusual for him not to get his own way about most everything. He scowled at her.

'There was damn all I could do about it. It's written, and can't be erased. But so is the rest of it. I'm not entirely excluded from that foolish couple's Jives. Honestly, it's sickening to see him mooning after her like a cunt-struck boy! At his age, too! He must be all of three hundred and seventy!'

'Don't be bitchy!' she scolded playfully. 'Now you will be able to watch him aging. Think of that and be pleased. No more delaying time for him, or her. How come you didn't know about all this right from the start?'

'I'm the bad angel, remember? Certain things are kept from me and I have to crawl to people like Michael to get answers.'

She settled her shapely limbs beside him on the divan in his spacious chamber. The walls kept changing colour, from pink to flame, blue to sombre grey, the green of spring and the chestnut of autumn. There was a huge screen where films of a pornographic nature were constantly playing. Lovely, generous breasted woman and strapping men with huge cocks performed lewd acts that involved arse-fucking and whipping, bondage and gags, cunnilingus and fellatio.

Lucifer yawned. He needed greater stimulation and Aphrodite's busy brain was devising entertainment. She clapped her hands and two teams of high-stepping girls attired as ponies pranced in, drawing lightweight chariots. They were driven by grooms, naked apart from loin-clothes, who leapt down and restrained the high-strung fillies. Wearing nothing except leather girths, reins and with iron bits in their mouths, their hair was long and thick, resembling manes, and beautiful tails were thrust into their arse-holes. They pawed the ground in high-wedged boots, tossed their heads and whinnied.

The reception room became transformed into a racing track, forming a huge oval in an amphitheatre that resembled the Coliseum in Ancient Rome.

'Shall we race?' Aphrodite asked.

'A wager?' His eyes lit up and his boredom vanished. 'What shall it be?'

'You have the advantage there. Nothing I can offer will match your stake.' She had already wished her garments away and now wore the short kilt, metal breastplate, helmet and armbands of a charioteer, sandal-boots encasing her lower legs.

He conjured up a magnificent necklace and dangled it before her. 'This once belonged to the Queen of Sheba. In return, you can agree to follow my commands for the next six months.'

'Don't I always?' she asked wryly.

'Yes, but this may be something special.'

'Oh, very well.' She wanted to get him out of his gloomy mood. He was no fun when he was like this. 'But you'd better not cheat or Mother Lilith will deal with you.'

'Ha! You think I'm afraid of her?'

'She could make things uncomfortable.'

He, too, now wore the guise of a champion racer, similar to hers. He jumped on to the chariot that bounced under his weight and the girl in front took the strain on straps fastened to her arms and the staves. He flicked the whip over her bare shoulders, and she shivered and held her head high. He gathered the reins in his other hand, giving Aphrodite an impatient glance.

When she was ready they walked their steeds to the starting line, where one of the grooms stood, white handkerchief raised. He dropped it and the vehicles burst into actions. They shot round the track, neck and neck Lucifer didn't have it all his own way for Aphrodite was an experienced sportswoman, lighter than him and therefore putting less strain on the panting woman out front. She knew what she was suffering, having taken part as a pony girl on many occasions. The leather straps would be biting into her, the crupper rubbing between her legs, the boots heavy, the tail chaffing her rectum, and the whip biting wherever it fell, cutting into her skin, forming welts.

Aphrodite showed no mercy. She wanted the Queen of Sheba's necklace. She steered her chariot closer to Lucifer's so that the wheels grated together for an instant and then broke free. He glared at her and swore, lashed out with his whip and laid it across her back. The thong caught her bare upper arms and she cursed him in return. It had cost her time and now she was dropping back with him streaking ahead. They finished the first round with Aphrodite a length behind. Two more to go, and the 'ponies' were already flagging.

She applied her whip vigorously working it back and forth across the delectably wobbling buttocks and this had the desired affect. Her steed leaped forward and Lucifer, whipping his girl mercilessly, managed to keep up. The second round was completed and the third and last stretched ahead. Aphrodite could tell that her pony was exhausted. All the spirit had gone from her and she kept on stubbornly, but without any verve. Lucifer was having the same trouble with his, but he simply raised his arm and brought it down with full force, striking her repeatedly.

They reached the finishing post together, and he leapt to the ground, had the groom free the girl and then bend her over and sodomised her. Aphrodite was excited, too, and she beckoned the other groom and lay flat on her back on the chariot and ordered him to penetrate her and bring her to orgasm.

When she was satisfied, she pushed him away and rose. Lucifer had also taken his pleasure and dismissed the girl with a stinging slap to her rump. The scene changed to a balcony overlooking his city.

'It seems that neither of us won,' he said, an arm draped idly around her shoulders. 'You smell sweaty. We will bathe together.'

Slaves were already running about, filling the large sunken tub with scented water and tossing in a lavish abundance of rose petals. Aphrodite, naked now, lowered herself in it, luxuriating in the warmth and perfume. Lucifer was beside her.

She looked into his wolf's eyes and said, 'What would you have me do, master?'

'Come to Dirk's wedding. I'm sure that between us we can cause mayhem. It will be a day long remembered, or maybe not if I decide to banish remembrance.'

Gina put a cup of tea on the bedside table, then drew back the curtains, singing, 'Happy the bride the sun shines on today.'

Kirsty came fully awake, joy flooding her heart. It really was her wedding day!

Everything had gone so smoothly that she was almost afraid to believe it. Her mother, Tony and little brother Peter had arrived and booked into *The Admiral's Arms* as Andy and Alec were occupying the guestroom in the cottage. It was wonderful to see Val, and to feel that Tony was OK and accept Peter. In fact she loved him on sight, her only regret being that he wasn't her real sibling, only half a one.

She had not bothered with a hen-night, feeling it was all too passé, and Dirk, having so few friends, had not even thought about a stag do, though Lucifer expressed disappointment. There was nothing he enjoyed more than the upset, confusion and expense of a night spent with 'the boys'. It consisted of men behaving badly, getting drunk, hiring strippers and whores and, the so-called buddies of the groom, leaving him tied up somewhere with his trousers down.

There was one fly in the ointment, however. Kirsty had decided to let her father know and, to her chagrin, he had insisted on being there. 'I want to do my duty and give you away,' he had said down the phone.

'Dad, no one is "giving me away". I'm my own woman. We're not living in the dark ages when a father literally "gave" his daughter to another man. It's very tribal and I don't agree with it. Women aren't chattels to be passed from hand to hand.'

This tirade stopped him in his tracks. 'Steady on there, old girl. Get down off your Woman's Lib soapbox. All right, I won't do anything you don't like, but can Nicky and I come to the reception, if not the actual wedding? What about this Handfasting nonsense?'

'There you go, you see, condemning something that you know nothing about. If you're going to take that attitude, I don't want to talk about it.' Now Kirsty remembered why she had been so glad when her parents separated. He was quite impossible. Blinkered, self-opinionated, controlling and convinced that he was always right.

'A ridiculous pagan carry-on. I suppose Val has encouraged you.' His voice always took on a sneering tone when he mentioned his former wife.

'It has nothing to do with her. All this was decided before I got in touch. And I'd rather you and Nicky didn't come if you're going to be unpleasant to her and Tony.'

'Has she brought the brat?'

'Yes, and he's great.'

'Disgusting. Having a baby at her age.'

'I thought that you and Nicky were trying for one.'

'That's different.'

Knowing that it was no use arguing, Kirsty had reluctantly agreed that he should come to Rosewood Manor for the wedding reception and then replaced the phone in its cradle.

She thought about this as she showered and smoothed body lotion into her skin. She wanted every inch of her to be like satin for the enjoyment of her bridegroom. Shivers ran down her spine as she thought about Dirk.

They had deliberately stayed apart for twenty-four hours, bowing to tradition, and she couldn't wait for the wedding night. It would be spent at the manor, and next day they would fly to Bermuda for their honeymoon.

Gina hovered in attendance, helping Kirsty prepare for her big day. She and Andy would be there as witnesses and Seth was best man. Andy stuck his head around the bedroom door, his face plastered in moisturizer and a small towel covering his loins.

'Oh, girl, isn't this exciting?' He grabbed up tissues from the box on the dressing-table and dabbed his cheeks. 'Shaving is such a drag. I always have to use gallons of moisturiser afterwards. I'll wear foundation, mascara and the lot today. Mustn't let you down, must we, darling?'

'You always look amazing.' She was applying eye-shadow to her lids.

'I got on like a house on fire with your Mum, but I don't think Daddy approved of me when we met last evening.'

'He wouldn't. He's homophobic.'

'Is he really? You could have fooled me. I thought I caught the tiniest hint of a closet gay there.'

'My father? Gay? I don't think so, Andy.' Kirsty relaxed as Gina brushed her hair with long, sweeping strokes before fixing the fragrant flower wreath in place.

'I'm rarely wrong, girl. Bet you a quid that he's on both buses.' Andy nodded sagely and, leaning towards the mirror, borrowed her mascara brush and added another layer to his curling lashes.

Although Kirsty had risen early to prepare, the time seemed to rush by and before long a white limousine arrived to carry her and Gina to the register office in the high street. A crowd had gathered to wish her well, for she was becoming known and accepted. It was a fine building, given to the town by one of the former landowners, and many events took place there, including the recording of births, marriages and deaths.

In a happy daze, Kirsty entered the foyer to be met by her mother and Tony, with Peter in the background, minded by Meg. He was very proud of his carnation button-hole. Wearing her brilliant but unusual wedding gown, with her hair festooned with leaves and blossoms, Kirsty walked into the room where the civil ceremony would take place, and all she could see was Dirk.

She went through the routine, saying 'yes' in the right places, exchanging the rings that were passed over by Seth, and then signing the forms that would make her alliance with Dirk legal and binding. They were showered with confetti as they left, and those who had been invited followed the limousine away from the town.

The sun shone on the lovers, and the scene was mystical as they were soon in the stone circle where the priest and priestess awaited them. Meg had already introduced them and there had been a practice run-through, but it was nothing like the solemnity that now enfolded them. The followers, a selection of ladies wearing scarlet gowns and flowers in their unbound locks, gathered around with men who were also wearing appropriate robes. There was singing and pipes and drums and poetry, laughter and joy and best wishes for the couple.

Kirsty stood in the centre with her fingers linked in Dirk's, and the priestess waved incense over them to dismiss memories of other lovers from their minds and bodies. The priest brought over a candle, holding it before them as a symbol of their passion, words and responses were given, and then their hands were bound together with a wide red ribbon. Finally, they jumped over a lighted fire to seal the bond. Those who had witnessed their union were enthusiastic, and Val started to cry.

'It was so beautiful,' she sobbed, while her husband held her. 'I wish we had done that, Tony.'

'It's never too late,' Meg reminded. 'I expect my circle could arrange it before you go back to the States.'

Kirsty was deliriously happy, and Dirk invited everyone, including the Goddess Temple worshippers, to the reception at the manor. It seemed that nothing could mar that wonderful occasion.

'What a load of crap!' Lucifer exclaimed nastily, as he and Aphrodite witnessed the scene, though invisible to everyone else. They were outside the stones, unable to penetrate such a sacred place, much to his chagrin.

He was wearing a superb suit of Italian design, very suitable for a wedding breakfast, while she had on a chiffon dress, clingy though ladylike, and a broad-brimmed organza hat, similar to those worn by English royalty at garden parties. Fragile stockings and high-heeled court shoes completed the illusion of good breeding. She could carry it off very well, if she tried, and today it amused her to do so and also to pretend that she was Lucifer's fiancée.

They were being received by the bride and groom in the Great Hall of the manor. 'How gorgeous you're looking, my dear.' Lucifer raised Kirsty's hand to his lips, those wild animal eyes staring into hers. 'And you, too, Dirk. I never thought I'd see the day.'

Dirk gave a chilly smile, and introduced him to the other guests as 'Lucian'. The ladies were charmed by him, even those from the temple, and Val was impressed as he spoke knowledgeably to her and Tony about America and their life there.

He began with compliments. 'Kirsty's mother? You can't be! I thought you were her sister!' And including her ex in the conversation with, 'How could you have left such a lovely woman?' He didn't add 'for this', but the look he gave Nicky said it all.

She bristled. 'And what do you mean by that?'

'Nothing, my dear. Nothing at all.' Having dripped poison into her ear, he now left it to fester.

The atmosphere between the two couples was decidedly frosty. Lucifer baited Kirsty's father and his wife, a not very intelligent bimbo who was beginning to show her age. It took very little effort to have him and Val at each other's throats; under the cover of extreme politeness. Tony was soon involved, and Nicky let herself down by using bad language.

Lucifer's eagle eye had already noted everybody there, searching out their weaknesses, the rivalries that existed under the surface, the jealousies and ambitions. Though urbane and suave, there was little he liked more than causing ripples, apart from stirring up trouble between politicians and quarrelsome sects and warring factions.

Barend had helped to book the caterers and florists and the house was at its superb best.

Lucifer and he were old acquaintances, though he was remaining with his master, Dirk, one of the Undead who would live until doomsday. Therefore Lucifer would always have an ally in Dirk's establishment, wherever he decided to live. He shrugged when he thought about it - after all, it was written in the Great Record, wasn't it?

The disagreements among the guests were subdued, but seemed to pollute the atmosphere and soon even the people from the temple were arguing about trivialities.

Lucifer made sure the unrest spread like a canker through the reception, whispering to Aphrodite, 'I'm relying on them, darling. British to the marrow and hating to upset the equilibrium. It will bubble underneath, but all will be as polite as can be... in public.'

Aphrodite smiled at him admiringly. 'You're a clever devil, aren't you?'

'That's my job. Now, watch this.'

The reception was no longer sedate. Under the influence of champagne and Lucifer's will, it had degenerated into a drunken orgy. Dirk recognised the demonic dabbling of his former master, and cursed him roundly, unable to stop it. To his horror he watched highly respectable men and women behaving with complete abandon. Hats awry, expensive dresses in disarray, ladies who were stalwart members of the WI, were acting like harlots.

The sedate small orchestra that had been playing background music was banished, to be replaced by the hectic beat of a rock band. Those who were sober enough to stand were gyrating wildly, while others fell to the floor and tried to copulate.

'I adore such functions, Mr and Mrs Norman Normal letting their hair down and losing their inhibitions,' Lucifer remarked to Dirk, leaning on the gallery rail, staring at the dancing, fornicating crowd below.

'You've been determined to spoil my wedding, haven't you?' Dirk growled, worried for Kirsty. 'Why don't you bugger off to the Infernal Regions and leave me alone?'

'Oh, I will. Never fear. You can't begrudge me a little sport, can you? Don't worry, they won't remember anything about this, though the unrest between Kirsty's parents will go on simmering and I can hardly be blamed for that.'

By the time Dirk reached the bottom of the stairs, all had been returned to normal. The string quartet played on serenely. The guests were no more than a trifle merry, their clothing was in place, and not a single hint of impropriety to be seen. Kirsty's relatives were still at daggers drawn, but this was to be expected. Everyone said what a lovely wedding it had been.

'At last!' Dirk carried Kirsty over the threshold of the Master Bedchamber and deposited her on the four-poster. 'I thought it would never end.'

'All those people, and my parents being horrid to one another,' she murmured, hardly able to take in that they were alone, a married couple in their own private nuptial chamber, no one to interrupt or disturb them. They could spend hours there, and that was all she wanted to do.

'I'm sure it was a great success. They said how much they enjoyed it. I'm glad you didn't get involved. It was Lucifer's doing, you know. He enjoys stirring troubled waters.' He sat beside her and gently unfastened the flowers from her hair, coiling the curls around his fingers.

'I suspected as much. As soon as he arrived I knew he was up to something.'

'Stop worrying. We're married and the night is ours.'

'When did he go? I didn't see Aphrodite and him leave.' She was still apprehensive, expecting them to turn up at any moment.

'He did one of his vanishing acts and took her with him. By that time the champagne had been flowing and no one cared much any more if they were friends or enemies.'

'Mum's taken over the cottage, with Andy and Alec. And Dad's gone back to London in a huff. Gina caught my bouquet, you know.'

'She'll marry Seth. He's the salt of the earth. But forget about them... forget about everyone. I want you to think of no one but me... Mrs Stratten.'

That was her name now. She was starting to believe it. They had a whole lifetime before them. She was impatient to join her body with his, and caressed his face with her fingertips, then parted her lips to receive his tongue. Every time he kissed her it was like a new experience. Even in her early days with Martin, she had never known such exquisite sensations. It was impossible to wait any more. She ground her body against his, and then started to undress him. He assisted and was soon stripped to the buff. She tore at her own garments, though he had to help her with the lacing on the red basque. Then they lay there admiring one another with eyes and hands.

He fondled her nipples and ran his fingers past her waist and belly and she opened her legs so that no bit of her would be hidden from him. Her heart was thudding and every nerve responding as he parted her labial wings and exposed the pink pearl of her clitoris. He lowered his head, his hair brushing her upper thighs, and she felt his tongue licking and sucking, rousing and teasing her organ. She stiffened, lifted her hips towards that tantalising mouth, and his fingers dabbled in her dew and anointed her love-channel. She was oh-so ready for him, but first he brought her to a mind-shattering orgasm. At the height of it, when waves of feeling were pouring over her, he poised above her and thrust with his pelvis, driving his cock into her depths, harder and faster until it jabbed against her cervix.

She clasped her arms around his neck, holding him closer and closer, wanting them to become one person. As this was impossible, she did the next best thing, skin chaffing skin, sweat mingling with sweat, sexual juices mixing. She felt of no importance compared with the might of his passion and the strength of him. A man who had lived long but in a suspended state, never aging, never weakening, but now he was mortal and they must treasure each moment for one day their bodies would die and they would pass into the spirit world.

His pace quickened and he hammered into her as she rode him on an uprush of desire. His strong thrusts pierced her so profoundly that she felt as if she had been speared. Bliss flooded her as she ground her clit against his cock base at every inward stroke, hearing the slippery wet sounds of his urgent possession. She came again in a welter of intense pleasure and his climax had the force of a huge wave washing over her.

Waves! Massive waves pounding the deck of the ship, the ripped sails flying from the masts under the fury of the hurricane. The deck sloped at a perilous angle, the sailors, skeletal thin and haggard, added their voices to the uproar, wailing shanties as they struggled to control ropes and rigging.

Kirsty was soaked, her hair streaming and bedraggled, her naked body lashed by the spite of the hissing rain. Not only that - a whip was landing on her shoulders and back, snakelike, merciless, wielded by the tall dark figure who kept his balance without effort, his laughter mixing with the roar of the storm. Lucifer! She heard him shouting.

'You must keep your side of the bargain! You too, Dirk! I was promised sport in return for my favour. At the height of a vicious storm, I shall transport you back to your haunted ship where you'll watch me taking Kirsty in any way I want.'

'It's true! Recorded! Inevitable!' Aphrodite screeched, flying madly over the wrecked vessel, her draperies mingling with the wind. The Lilam were with her, those unholy sisters, demon-daughters of Lilith, Lucifer's consorts.

Kirsty knew there was nothing she could do. Dirk, helpless, was chained to the wheel, but couldn't control the ship. He was forced to watch as Lucifer flogged her, then swept her up so that she was suspended between the deck and the storm clouds. Lightning flashed, great jagged forks, terrifying in their intensity and she thought she was about to die. But Lucifer hung there, within Dirk's sight, turning Kirsty towards him and thrusting between her thighs, drawing up her legs so that they scissored around his neck.

'Stop! Stop!' Dirk's voice was lost in a massive thunderclap.

Aphrodite straddled him, pushing her pubis into his face, silencing him and riding him to completion, her sisters jostling to take her place and bring themselves pleasure on any portion of his body that they could reach. Their screams of ecstasy reverberated in the chaos, their mighty orgasms becoming a part of the violent storm.

Lucifer held Kirsty poised beneath him, and then fell into her, impaling her on his enormous cock. She yelled with pain, yet her core had never been so thoroughly penetrated, stirring pleasure in her depths, his phallus a freezing pole driving into her centre. He lifted her up and down on it, and the root of that icy weapon butted against her clitoris. Her vagina felt hot, yet it did not melt his organ into warmth, its girth rubbing her G-spot, its stem butting against her nubbin.

Pain and desire racked her. She clung to the thought of Dirk, her beloved husband, but Lucifer's thrusts brought on her climax and just as she came, she stared into his blazing eyes and was filled with dread. She could never escape from the bargain she had made with him. His essence flooded into her and she screamed as he let her fall to the deck.

Abruptly the storm abated, the clouds parted and the first orange rays of dawn spread across the sky. Kirsty was standing by Dirk, and the demon women had disappeared. Lucifer stood in the shrouds, staring down at the couple.

'Look for me,' he shouted, his lips curved in that sardonic smile. 'Twice a year you will sail with me, just as you used to do, Dirk. And you, Kirsty, will pleasure me.'

She shivered but weighed up the advantages. She had saved Dirk and would love him until death, a natural death at a time written in the Akashic Record. Yet she challenged Lucifer, 'Why should I do that?'

His laughter rang out, rising about the sound of the ocean and nature as he bellowed, 'It's part of the bargain!'

The sun slanted through the gap in the heavy drapes hanging at the bay window. It struck across Kirsty's face and she woke. Dirk was asleep beside her and she snuggled against his chest, breathing in his warmth, and relishing the fact that this was the morning after their wedding day and that they were going on their honeymoon.

She sat up, feasting her eyes on the man she loved so much and, gradually, fragments of her dream impinged on her happiness. The ghost ship! The storm! And Lucifer! He had come to claim his reward and she had yielded to him. She rather dreaded Dirk waking for he would remember. Those wild women, Aphrodite and her sisters. They had had their way with him.

He was stirring, smiling at her. 'Darling, you're here,' he murmured sleepily. Then his eyes sharpened. 'The ship! We were there! And he had you!'

'Yes, yes, but look what we have in return.'

She left the bed and walked to the window, pushing open the casement. The garden sparkled with dew, and there wasn't a cloud in the sky. Had it been a real storm or an astral one? Since arriving in Cornwall the veil between worlds had grown thin and things once incredible now happened almost mundanely.

But why me? She asked across the ether. *Lucifer, why do you want me?*

And a voice whispered in her ear, so close that she jumped. 'Just for the Hell of it!'

Thanks for reading!

Have you read Rhea Silva's **FOR ALL TIME**? If not, it's also available as a paperback from **AMAZON**.

He whipped off her scarf and covered her eyes. She stiffened and tried to remove it, but he captured her hands. Deprived of sight and restrained by his iron grip, it seemed as if her other senses had sharpened. She could smell the candles and his aftershave. He pushed up her T-shirt, and she heard and felt the zipper of her jeans running down. Then he bore her back until hard stone chilled her bare spine. He stretched her arms out on either side, and there was a click as cuffs were fastened to her wrists and then attached to chains. She couldn't move.

Freya Mullin, an authority on ancient buildings, is to survey Daubeney Manor, which has recently been purchased by Maxwell Sinclair, an authority on cults and temples and old religions.

Baffled by Maxwell's arrogant refusal to take her into the subterranean passages, she goes there secretly, accompanied by a long-time friend. To their surprise they find an ancient, orgiastic temple that appears to have been occupied recently.

Maxwell does not want to share the temple with anyone, intending to use it for his own Hell Fire Club, and Freya has no idea of the twists and turns of fate that will now involve her as she becomes ever more entangled in his ambitions.